Killing Eva

~

Camellia Hart

Cover design by Camellia Hart ©

Self-published

ISBN 978-0-9976705-4-7

www.CamelliaHart.com

Killing Eva is a work of fiction. Names, characters, places, and incidents either are the product of the author's imagination or are used fictitiously. Any resemblance to actual persons, living or dead, business establishments, events, or locales is purely coincidental.

To my amazing editor...

Chapter 1

"Nine-one-one, what's your emergency?"

"Yes, hi. Ahh…this lady…she's bleeding. She might have been shot."

"Could you provide your location, sir?"

"I'm on the 101 to Pacifica."

"Thank you. Is she conscious?"

"N-no. She's…ahh…let me check. Oh! Oh God, she's not breathing. There's no pulse. She's dead. She's dead!"

"Sir, please, calm down. I'm sending you help. Now, are you related to the woman?"

"What? No! I don't know her. I found her…on the side of the freeway. It's raining, and when I saw this car, with lights on, but no one inside—look, I'm only trying to help."

"I appreciate you calling us, sir. Help is on the way. Please, could you stay in your car until they arrive?"

Chapter 2

"Wow!" Eva skated a few feet away from the ski lift chair toward the beginning of the trail but came to an abrupt halt at the first sight of Lake Tahoe's sapphire blue water glistening against the pristine, snow filled slope that sprawled ahead of her.

"Yes, wow." Clive placed a soft kiss on her cheek.

The way he looked at her, it wasn't the lake he complimented. Even in the icy cold of the high elevation, Eva's face heated to Clive's adoration. How much she loved this man. His kiss reminded her of their first kiss, in his bedroom on that New Year's Eve, in his parents' home in Sausalito. How much her life had changed since then. Her parents' divorce had led her away from Clive for a long fifteen years, only for her to meet him again in the very building her father's office, S. F. Designs, had been in all the while. Clive had told her once, had she not taken the helicopter ride with him to Santa Barbara, he would have pursued her however long it would take to make her go out with him. Such was Clive. An intense, powerful, persistent man who'd get what he desired, by will or might, and in her case, by love. Nothing could tear them apart. She wouldn't allow it. He wouldn't allow it.

"Ready?" Carter angled the ski poles he'd pierced into the snow, preparing for a forward push.

They gave Clive's brother a nod and turned to their friends to confirm.

"Not yet." Allie screeched and bit into her lower lip.

Eva couldn't tell why her best friend would take up a challenge knowing she'd fail. Like that time Allie prepared to jump off the dock into the lake, of course, her feet slipped on the edge. Of course, she fell on her behind and bounced into the water. Or like that time she'd prepared to trim her waist-length red hair, of course, the stylist sneezed just as she had been about to make that first snip. Of course, Allie cried for months about her short bob. And then that time she prepared to chug a full glass of beer...

Allie didn't look one bit confident in the challenges she'd set herself up for then, nor did she now. *Why the sudden need to impress Marc?* He loved Allie years before Allie found out that he loved her. Before he could muster the courage to ask her to prom, she went with someone else. Before he could ask her to go out with him, she'd already started to date someone else. And when he did go out with her, before he could ask her to marry him, she'd already decided to refuse. But Allie did agree to marry Marc in the end. Had that been why she attempted this feat? To make up for all those times Marc had been a step ahead of her?

Marc crouched in front of Allie and tugged the strings on her snowboard boots. "How's that?" He looked up at her, his smile filled with adoration for Allie.

"Much better." She grinned.

Not a real grin. Izzy stared at Eva and shook her head. The numerous times Izzy, Eva's other best friend, looked at her that way after something Allie did. When Allie bounced into the water, when Allie cried about her haircut, when Allie chugged that beer.

Marc placed a quick kiss on Allie's leg and moved on to fixing the other boot.

Izzy pushed her skis and slid to Eva. Eva cut a quick look at Allie, hoping Allie hadn't witnessed Izzy's disapproval. She hadn't.

Izzy leaned in as though for only Eva to hear. "She snowboards now?" Her voice, though a conspiratorial whisper, still seemed a bit loud, and Eva cut Allie yet another glance. "I mean, after the many times she talked me out of taking snowboarding lessons, claiming I'll cause her emotional distress."

"What?" Clive's brows shot together.

"Shh. Come closer." Izzy waved her gloved hand.

And he did.

Eva tilted her head to Izzy, giving her a what-are-you-doing glare.

"You know I deserve to feel this way, Eva."

"You should have taken that lesson anyway."

"Well…" She shot Allie a hesitant glance. "I did."

"And?"

"And, Allie's right. But that's not the point."

Clive leaned into their conversation, exposing a level of curiosity, that until now, Eva hadn't known existed—apparently her tall, sexy lover liked gossip—he looked unfazed.

Izzy rolled her eyes. "She claims I'll just sit there, in her way, obstructing her skiing experience." She leaned farther in toward Eva and Clive. "But now that Marc snowboards, she snowboards?"

"Okay. We're ready now." Allie gave them another one of her halfhearted grins. But then she moved and, in slow motion, Allie tilted forward and fell flat on her face.

Eva held back a chuckle, but Izzy threw her head back and laughed aloud. A few birds bolted into the sky from a nearby pine, away from them, away from Izzy.

"I'm definitely recording this." Izzy tugged at the Velcro closure on her coat pocket to pull out her phone but stopped halfway at Allie glaring at her as though ready to shatter the phone to pieces.

"Why don't we get started and do a few runs, while"—Clive gave Allie his signature megawatt grin—"Marc turns you into a pro snowboarder?"

That got Allie to smile. A genuine smile.

Because who could resist Clive's charm? The same charm that reeled Eva closer and closer to him every second she spent with him. The same charm that made her want to pinch herself to ensure it hadn't all been a dream. That he had asked her to marry him. That she had agreed.

She pushed the fingers of her left hand deeper into the glove and the metal of her engagement ring rubbed against her skin.

Real.

Her longing for him, her love for him was all so real, her eyes stung from the emotions that tightened her chest, warming her, soothing her, exciting her about all that the future would hold for her and Clive.

Something in Clive's expression confirmed similar thoughts raced his mind. He pulled her near for another kiss. She tilted her head, angling her cheek, but he reached for her lips.

"Can't wait to do it."

At the exaggerated seriousness in his voice, laced with mischief in his expression, his innuendo unmistakable, she exhaled a light laugh. Of course, he also meant he couldn't wait to ski with her for the very first time.

"Ready?" He grinned and pulled down his goggles. As though a punishment for her relentless gawking the sensual visual of his greenish-blue irises were replaced by an opaque iridescent lens that displayed her reflection. Her heart crumbled. She could never have enough of this guy.

She gave him a light nod, and then they started

to ski down the groomed slope.

Freezing wind blasted at her as she sped. But the bright sun provided the right amount of warmth to cut through the cold. The crisp fragrance of lush pine trees tickled her nostrils, awakened her senses, and brought back sweet memories from all the times she'd been on this slope. Many times with her family, a few times with her friends. Each time her skis cut the crusty snow, excitement and joy filled her. And to think she'd share this all with the love of her life. Clive met her speed and crisscrossed the trail she'd left behind. She let her smile linger on her face, because really, she couldn't have wished for a better day.

They reached the end of the slope, and seconds after Izzy and Carter followed. Knowing Allie and Marc would be nowhere close to them, they queued at the end of a long line to get on the chairlift that would take them back to the top of the trail.

"Too many people here today," Carter grumbled as he shuffled ahead.

"I was thinking the same. We should try the Nevada side," Clive suggested.

"Let's." Izzy, too, shuffled ahead.

"Maybe we do a few more runs here so Allie and Marc can catch up?" As Eva said that, the chair arrived, and they got on. Clive held her gloved hand in his through the entire ride up the mountain. A thing they did now all the time, and yet, their togetherness sent waves of happiness through her. She tightened her grip and he pulled her hand into his lap.

They skied down the slope a couple more times.

The first time Eva passed Allie, she waved at her friend.

Allie attempted to wave back but fell flat on her face.

That definitely hurt.

The second time Eva passed the run, she met Marc. "Where's Allie?"

He pointed with a gloved finger.

She shot her gaze in that direction and found Allie lying in the snow, again, face down.

And the last time Eva passed Allie, she caught her hiking down the slope. Allie stomped into the rental shop and disappeared, while they gathered near the ski lift and waited for her. Minutes later, Allie returned. Snowboard gone, she threw a pair of skis down on the snow. "Well, at least I tried." She pushed one boot into the groove and snapped on the ski. Repeated the same with the other.

"Guess I can take those snowboarding lessons now." Izzy said to Allie.

"Thought you already did. And, I was right, you totally sucked."

Per Clive's plan, they got onto the chairlift to traverse from California to the Nevada side of the mountain.

Clive pulled down the protective bar and read the attached trail map.

"This is where we want to go." He pointed the location with his finger. "One thing, though, see how this forks into two? You want to go this way." He swiped his finger along the trail he'd intended them to stay on. "And not down here, which is through the trees and off the trail. It's beautiful, but they rarely groom this piece. It's a steep drop at the beginning, and if you aren't careful you'll tumble right down. So, let's avoid that and go this way, to the left. Okay?"

Yep.

"Where are Trevor and Tina? Weren't they supposed to join us?"

"Yeah, let me call him." Clive pulled one hand out of the glove and brought his phone out from his jacket pocket. He dialed his friend Trevor.

"Hey man, where are you? … Okay. We're heading to Nevada. … Okay. See you there. … What? Oh yeah, tell Tom to join us there."

Eva stepped out of the ski lift and slid a few meters down the slope to an overlook. Clive had it right; there were fewer people on this slope. Other than them, a couple of teenagers, and a family of four, the starting point of the trail was deserted. Eva glanced at the lift. A few empty chairs rolled by, then one carrying a man dressed in all black approached.

The man began to ski off the lift on to the mountain when Carter asked, "Let's go?"

Eva swiveled around to face the slope. "Let's."

"Stay to the left." Clive reminded.

Just as they began to descend, a feminine voice caught Eva's attention. "Excuse me."

Eva jerked to a halt and looked over her

shoulder.

The woman had called out to Clive. "Please, could you take a picture for us?"

"Sure." Clive took a pocket-size camera from the woman and cut Eva a quick glance. "Go ahead. I'll catch you."

Eva gave him a nod but continued to gaze at the family of four gathering for the group photo. She'd posed like that many times with her family, with her mother, her brother, and her father—in that exact spot where this family stood.

Clive shot her one more look, and right away brought down the camera as though the family wasn't waiting for him to take their picture, his expression readable.

Before he could ask what was wrong, she nodded again, drew in a deep breath to stabilize her thoughts as she faced the trail, and began skiing down the slope, following her friends.

Eva and her father were avid skiers. Her mother skied only to please her father, and her brother skied only for the hot chocolate. Because it wasn't just any hot chocolate; when her mother wasn't looking, her father would pull out a tiny flask and pour a shot of alcohol into Joey's mug. She smiled as that visual passed her mind. Those were happy days. And these days were too, with Clive and her friends. They should take a group photo from that overlook when they went back up for their next run.

Oh shit.

She had passed the section of the trail that forked

in two directions and absentmindedly drifted toward the wrong run. The only way to recover would be a sharp turn to the left. She maneuvered her skis to do just that, when from the corner of her eye, she glimpsed a shadow of someone, or something. Bears did roam these slopes. She flinched and before she could recover from her shock, that someone or something shoved. Hard. Aggressive. She lost her balance. She fell. Off the cliff, down the trail Clive had warned her to stay away from. She dove sideways a few meters off the sharp drop, till she hit the powdery snow, and tumbled farther along the steep slope. One of her skis dislodged and stayed behind while the other remained stuck to her boot and twisted her knee. An excruciating pain darted through her leg each time she rolled and skidded down the trail. She cringed in agony each time her knee met the ground and deepened the twist in an awkward angle.

Though it seemed like she'd been falling for eternity, it also happened so fast, when she came to a stop, everything around her turned dark. She panted. She gasped. And when she tasted snow, it occurred to her that she lay face down. *Like Allie.* A light laugh escaped her.

But humor disappeared when she pressed her gloved palm flat on the snow and pushed the ground to turn over. A difficult maneuver, given all energy had been sucked out of her from the fall. The rollover corrected the position of the one ski that remained stuck to her boot. She lay still. Blinked at the sky, tinted pink through her goggles. She drew in a deep breath. And held it there. Pain emerging from the pit of her stomach radiated and consumed every inch of her body. Her kneecap throbbed. She rubbed the area to soothe, but it did nothing.

What just happened? Who the hell was that? A bear? Shoving her like that? Maybe not. Clive? No. Can't be. He'd always been gentle with her. He would never nudge her for fun, let alone shove her down the slope he'd insisted she avoid. Maybe he lost his balance and bumped into her? Or it must have been Allie. She lost control, again, thanks to her idiot snowboarding obsession. No. Allie had switched to skis. So, not Clive. Not Allie. Someone else. Someone else… Her insides did a quick tumble at that thought. She shot up to a seated position. Unintentional? Deliberate? But who?

Two black skis skidded to a harsh halt ahead of her.

She tilted her head back, and her gaze met with the man dressed in all black she'd spotted earlier on the chairlift.

Deliberate. "What the hell is wrong with you?" she screamed.

"Me?" He chuckled. "Nothin'. You on the other hand, missy, are gonna get yourself killed if you don't listen very carefully to what I'm 'bout to say next."

The accent… *That* accent. Her gut tightened. *The informant.* The nerve of this guy. Wasn't it enough that he'd threatened her father until his death, and once Eva took over S. F. Designs, sent her threatening letters? He'd watched her when she went for a run in the park. He'd met her outside the coffee shop, posed as a reporter. One night, when she'd had girlfriends over, he came to her home, dropped off a note blackmailing her to break all ties with Clive.

She'd expected him to meet her, especially after Clive had announced Stanford Enterprises' continued partnership with S. F. Designs, effectively challenging the informant's latest threat. But, that he would make a move with all her friends and Clive around, seemed reckless even for this guy.

Feminine laughter echoed through the rustling trees. Startled but grateful, she turned her head sideways and glanced behind her. On the steep slope that would forever appear in her nightmares, she found no one. The voices must have come from above the ridge, the trail she was supposed to be on.

"Help!" she shouted the loudest she'd ever shouted. The word scorched her throat as it left her. "Hel—"

"Don't."

Something clicked, and her insides collapsed. Because that sound could mean only one thing.

She should scream. She couldn't. She should breathe. She couldn't. Her mouth dried out. Every inch of her body tightened. She sat frozen, not from the biting cold of the crusty ice she sat on, nor from the winter wind that gusted past her, but from the unexpected fear that had consumed her when she stared at the muzzle of the handgun pointed at her.

The warmth from the sun vanished. A sharp chill sprinted along her spine, and she trembled in her fleece insulated clothing.

"Clive will come looking for me," she mumbled her only hope as loud as she could, barely over a whisper.

He chuckled again. "I'll be long gone before he'll find you here. Besides, he's too busy playin' a photographer. The one time he should be protectin' his fiancée."

She hated his guts. But what could she do?

"And where's that bodyguard? Tom? Big man. Guess he's afraid to ski. Which means it's just you and me for now."

Though a balaclava, dark goggles, and a helmet masked his face, the laughter hidden in his tone gave away his arrogance. She riled. She wouldn't let him belittle Clive, or Tom for that matter. She wouldn't let him threaten her and get away. Not this time.

Because he feared too. He feared getting caught. Like that time when he'd met her by the coffee shop. Alarmed by Clive's call, he'd run away from her. When she'd chased after him in Central Park, again, he'd run away from her. When he'd come to her home to leave that threat letter, hearing Clive's voice on the intercom, he'd run away once more.

Her gaze drifted back to the handgun. He wouldn't shoot her. He said she'd get killed *if* she didn't listen. "What do you want?" she spoke through gritted teeth as her fight for survival strengthened.

The informant had it right. Clive would not get to her as fast as she hoped. Unless he'd seen her be pushed, in which case he should have already been here. Otherwise, he'd find her missing only after meeting with the rest of their friends. The soonest way to get to her would either be via the chairlift, and skiing down the steep cliff, or hitch a snowmobile ride with a ski patrol. Whichever method, he'd be with her in about seven to ten minutes. *Too long.* She had to fight this guy by herself.

With the slightest pressure of her thumbs she pressed the top of the ski poles she held in her hands and unhooked them from her gloves. She gripped the handles tight, readying for the opportune moment when she'd lunge up and swing them at him.

"Leave the company," he said. "You have…eh…one week."

Had he just made up the threat? Her newfound strength won over her otherwise rational, practical, sane mind. "Not gonna happen." Her heart jumped as the words left her lips. *What am I doing?*

He took a quick step forward, making the gun point that much closer to her. "Don't push me, Eva."

Yes, don't push him, you moron. "One week is too soon."

"Okay, how about one month?"

"And who's to take over after me?"

"You'll get one of them letters."

She tried hard not to seem bothered by the humor in his tone. "Why can't you tell me that now?"

He didn't answer.

"Why do you want me to leave the company?"

15

No answer.

"Is someone paying you to do this? I'll pay you double if you tell me who that is."

He took another quick step toward her and just as fast she jerked backward. She tightened her grip on her ski poles. Should she swing at him now?

His silence, his demeanor, not to mention that gun, shook her. Her nervousness took over, her palms grew sweaty inside her gloves. "Why are you following me? Did you follow my father too? Did you kill him?"

"I didn't kill your father," he snarled.

"Then who did?"

He didn't answer.

"I can get both of us out of this. Just tell me who it is."

"Don't. Push. Me."

The way he steadied his gun this time, he'd do it, he'd pull the trigger.

All words left her. She stared in disbelief. She wanted to be with Clive more than she'd ever wanted to be with him. Had she known that last kiss would be their last kiss… Her chest grew heavy with rising anguish. No. This is not how her life should end. No! Not here. Not today. Not like this. She wouldn't let it. She tightened her grip on her ski poles.

"One month. You can make all of this go away, just like that."

She stared at him, unmoving, ensuring he didn't sense what she was about to do.

He kept the gun pointed at her for a moment more and then moved his finger off the trigger.

Just as he did that, she sprang up, and in one hurried motion held both her poles together and swung them at him as hard as she could. As quick as she was, he lurched to one side and dodged her blow. She struck the gun instead and it slipped from his gloved fingers. The gun landed nearer to her than to him and sank into the powdery snow. She leaped for it and picked it up, but before she got to aim it at him, he'd already turned around and skied fast away.

Her chest hurt at how heavily she panted, but she continued to clutch the gun in her shaking hands, pointing it in the direction he'd gone. Not like he would hike back up the slope, but it did take an eerie screech from a large bird somewhere among the trees to alert her that he wouldn't return, and to think about what she should do next.

She set the gun next to her, on the ice, zipped open her jacket and pulled out her phone from the inside pocket.

Should she call Clive? Her finger hovered on speed dial. But he'd still be skiing down the slope unaware that she tried to reach him.

She dialed the next best person to handle the situation. "Tom." Still winded, she spoke slightly over a whisper, "Where are you?"

"Parking. What's wro—"

"Man. All black clothing. Black skis and helmet." She paused, only to draw in a much-needed breath. "Should be getting off the slope any minute now. He's the informant."

"I'll track him down."

Good, but… "He knows you."

"I see." Tom sounded grim. "Does he know Mike?"

The informant had spoken of her bodyguard, but in singular. Maybe he hadn't yet spotted the undercover security guy Clive had set up for her. "I don't think so. He named only you."

"Okay. We'll send Mike after him." He paused. "Eva, please tell me he didn't hurt you."

Rare for Tom to call her Eva. But he did on occasions when he worried for her the most. "I'm fine. He separated me from the rest of the group and, as always, he got lucky."

"Never again. I'll make sure of that." The fury in Tom's voice gave her the courage to move on from the incident, at least until she reconnected with Clive and her friends.

As Eva ended her call with Tom, her phone flashed with an incoming call from Clive.

"Where are you?"

And just like that, all the strength she'd gathered drained. Her emotions welled from hearing Clive's voice, from the worry in his tone, of his fear of losing her, of how much he loved her over everything and everyone else.

Her vision blurred from the tears that filled and stung her eyes. She shut them tight. Heavy warm drops trickled down her face and settled on the inside rim of her ski goggles. She tugged at the frame, stretched the elastic, and rested them over her helmet. The cold wind that brushed past her brought a sense of relief that, though only for this moment, her obstacle had abated. Her gaze fell to the gun next to her. She picked it up with a shaky hand.

"Eva, what happened?"

Dread in Clive's voice begged her to say something, anything, but where should she begin? How much should she say? And over the phone? Because even the slightest hint of her strained mental condition would shatter Clive further. He'd blame himself for it all.

She'd recount every detail of the incident to him, but in person, in a few minutes when she saw him again. She swallowed her sadness and brought control to her scattering thoughts.

"Took the wrong run. Heading down now. See you by the lift."

She tapped the End Call button before Clive could probe. He knew she hadn't told him everything. She'd terrified him. But that her phone didn't buzz meant he'd wait for when she would be ready to talk. Typical Clive. Doing it her way, even when it hurt him the most. Even in high stress he treated her with such patience and love. But her calm should give him hope that she was not in as much a terrible situation as he may have imagined.

Eva hiked up the steep mountain and collected her ski. She slid her shoes between the bindings. Ignoring the throbbing knee, she started down the slope.

Preoccupied from her dreary thoughts she remained unmindful of the difficulty of the terrain she maneuvered. She relived the encounter in her mind. Her insides rattled. Her heart bled. The reality of what had happened began to set in. She'd come face to face with death. The informant, his arrogant tone, the gun, the threat to her company, the one-month deadline, the entire horrific experience played like a movie in front of her eyes.

She descended down the path that connected her to the initial trail Clive had wanted her to take. Her awareness returned when she made a final turn toward the lift, and her gaze fell on Clive and her friends, gathered for her.

Clive pulled his phone away from his ear and slid it into his pants pocket, his hardened expression easy to read. He'd spoken to Tom. *He knows*.

She abandoned her skis, the poles, her helmet, and ran into his arms. He squeezed her tight against his chest. His heart pounded against her ear. Deprived of his familiar warmth since the moment she'd left him on top of the mountain, she breathed relieved and wilted into his protective embrace.

"I'm so sorry, Eva," he exhaled her name in a whisper filled with too much unwarranted regret.

She moved in closer and pressed deeper against his chest.

He nuzzled his face into her hair. "I shouldn't have asked you to go without me. I should have let you wait. I-I'm so, *so* sorry."

***

He inserted a small shiny microchip into his cell phone and dialed his employer's number. "It's done. I want my money now."

His employer's familiar rough grunt no longer affected him.

"It's done when I say it's done."

Usual for his employer to sound grouchy. Usual for him to wish he'd never taken this job. But he no longer wanted to play this game. "It. Is. Done." He mimicked his employers tone. That should get his message across.

But it didn't. Because silence.

"You said we were only threatenin' her. Which I've done plenty. What else do you need me for?"

Silence.

He cupped his hand over his jaw and covered one side of his mouth. "I kept my part of the deal. Now pay me, dammit," he whispered as loud as he could. In reality, he wanted to shout. And, though he sat away from the rest of the passengers, on the last seat of the skier commuter bus riding to the parking lot where he'd left his car, he couldn't risk any of them overhearing him. Given how well his plan to intimidate Eva had gone, he would be stupid to draw attention now. Maybe he should have waited until he'd gotten into his car to make this phone call. But he'd endured far too much from his employer. He needed to get paid…he needed to put an end to this job.

"I'll pay you."

His employers switch to a casual tone caught him off guard. There had to be a catch. "When?"

"When she leaves the company."

"No. You pay—"

"Tell me *exactly* how it went."

From the start, he'd hated every second of every conversation he had with his employer. It only seemed fair to plan revenge. That day, when they'd finally meet, that day, when he'd finally get paid, that day would be a terrible day for one of them. He smiled, imagining the last moments of his employer's life—moments the ingrate would spend begging him for forgiveness.

He narrated what had occurred between him and Eva. "Who is to take over after her?"

"That's none of your business."

"I told her she'd get another one of those notes. Am I delivering that?"

"Like I said, it's none of your business."

"Good. I'm done workin' for you anyway. All I want now is to get paid."

"And all I want now is for you to continue telling me exactly how it went."

He gritted his teeth at that bristling tone. Without thinking, he slipped and mentioned leaving the gun behind. Anticipating his employer's reaction, he winced even as the words left his mouth.

"You colossal idiot. How difficult would it have been to snatch it right back from her? Is it registered to you?"

He let that slide. Because, sure, he could explain every detail of his encounter with Eva, but more than anything else, he wanted to get paid. And something told him his employer had never intended to compensate him. "I want my money."

"Are you being followed?"

He knew it. She was never going to pay. *She?* Why did he think his employer was a woman? And being followed? "No!"

"Are you sure?"

He spun around and peeked outside the back window. "I don' think so."

"Son of a—" his employer shouted.

"What are you so worked up for? So what if someone's followin' me? I didn't do anything they can prove. Was just Eva and me. Nobody saw us."

His employer exhaled sharply.

He pulled the phone away from his ear.

"Do you have a place to stay, *other* than your damn boat?" his employer asked.

Not *his* damn boat. It belonged to his grandpa. Actually, it belonged to whomever his grandpa stole it from. A secret his grandpa shared only with him. It had become his hiding place all those times he'd run away from home. His mother's home, his childhood home, he hated that home. So, no, he didn't have a place to stay other than that damn boat.

"Why?" he asked.

"They are following you, *you idiot*."

He swiveled around in his seat once again and peeped through the rear window. A few cars trailed the bus, but none of the drivers resembled Eva's bodyguard, or her fiancé. Imagining either of them following him made an anxious fear dart down his spine. Maybe he shouldn't have mocked them to Eva? He scanned once more, slower this time, and examined the passengers inside the approaching cars. "I'm s-sure, I'm not being followed."

And silence.

"Hello? Are you there?"

"If you go to your boat before Eva leaves the company—you hear me? *Before* she leaves, if *you* go to *your* boat, I will not pay you. Ever."

"Where am I supposed to go then?" Not to Mama's house for sure. Besides, he never could stay there for more than a couple of hours.

Memories from his horrid childhood colored his mind dark. His father's drinking, his mother's shouting, their fighting, the blood that pooled under his father as he laid dead, his mother's regretless expression after she shot a bullet right through his father's chest.

His heartbeat rose to a painful pace. He pressed his palm flat against his chest to suppress the agony that welled from his reminiscence.

No. He couldn't stay at his mother's. Maybe a motel. But short on money, he'd waited for this gig to fill his pockets. "Pay me half now, and the remainder later."

"No."

"Listen, I need the money, okay?" His jaw hurt from how tight he clenched.

"You'll figure something out."

"No. I won't. You better pay me, bitch."

"What?" his employer barked. "What did you call me?"

"Asshole. Whatever. I don' know who you are, an' I don' really care. Give me my money, and I'm gone. I'm not waitin' a whole damn month."

And silence. Again.

He'd worked hard on this job. Eva had it right. He had followed her father. He didn't dislike the man. He seemed like a nice guy. And Eva too, he liked Eva. He liked her friends. He liked her life. His encounter today with Eva began to settle in. His heart shattered from the guilt of what he'd done. He would never do it again. He'd never threaten Eva again. He'd never follow her again. He hated that all this time she blamed him for her father's death. Good he'd cleared that up.

He'd better end his suffering once and for all. "I'm—" He cleared his throat, as though that could subside the rising guilt that had prepared to choke him dead. He exhaled in defeat. "I'll stay at my mama's house."

"Good. And I'll signal you when I have the money."

"Before the end of the month?"

"Yes."

"How?"

"You'll know when you see it." That usually irritable voice sounded eerily calm. He much preferred his employer angry.

"Guess I'll finally be meetin' you." How he waited for that moment.

"Don't call me again."

"What? Why not? You'd better pay me, you hear?" Silence. "Hey? You there?"

He tried to redial the number, but the call didn't go through. "What the—" he muttered, and tried, and retried to reach his employer.

"Fuck. Fuck!" He hit his phone against the back of the seat ahead of him.

A few passengers turned and looked his way. Among them all, his gaze settled on the man seated nearest to him, and he gave him his best deathly stare. But the guy did not flinch. He stared him down with matched vigor.

If only he still had that gun.

"Asshole," he mouthed from his balaclava-covered face without making a sound.

The guy turned back around.

Good. He smiled at his little victory.

He pulled out the microchip from his phone and snapped it in two. His anger lightened from the swift crack of the thin plastic, as though he'd snapped his employer's neck. Wrinkly neck? Not like that would matter. *She'd better pay me. She? Could be a he.*

He rehearsed in his mind his plan for when he'd meet his employer. Would his employer plead for mercy? To spare his life—*his* life, *her* life? It killed him that he hadn't found his employer's identity yet.

If only he knew who it was. Heat flushed through his body.

If only he knew, because he'd then have leverage to blackmail back. His muscles tightened to the point of pain.

If only he knew. He pulled his hands into fists and punched the back of the seat ahead of him. A light crack appeared where his fist had made contact.

That guy turned to look at him again, and this time he stood from his seat.

The fury he carried in this moment for his employer encouraged him to brawl with this guy. He pulled out his gloves, stretched his fingers back and forth, readying for a knockout punch.

But the bus came to a halt, and just like that, the guy stomped away in his ski boots and exited the bus.

He stared after the guy. His chest heaved. He took off his helmet and peeled back his balaclava. Chilled air crept from the open door and rushed to his face. The sweat that had begun to trickle from his hairline began to cool.

He dragged in a deep breath.

He would have killed the guy.

What's wrong with me?

Chapter 3

Eva stared at the crimson fire transforming into a large devilish flicker as it devoured the wood Clive had piled into the rustic stone fireplace.

The radiant heat, the dusky hue of dancing light cast around the room, the calming cross-legged yoga pose Eva sat in atop a fluffy pillow she'd set on the hardwood floor, the velvet throw she'd wrapped around her shoulders, the full-bodied red wine that awakened her taste buds each time she pulled in a long sip, all while being in company of loved ones, should have made for a memorable evening in the chalet. Yet, none of it mattered today. No level of material comfort could tear her away from the horrid thoughts that had blanketed it all.

One month—only thirty days—to leave behind all that her father had wanted her to own, to grow, to flourish. But whom would the note indicate to take over after her? It couldn't be someone she knew.

Could it? Why hadn't he told her who that was? Maybe he didn't know. Maybe who ever had been guiding him all this time hid this from him. And what if she wouldn't let go? She should have asked him that. Would she meet with the same fate as her father? A visual of her life ending in a hit and run accident flashed through her mind and—

"Eva?" Clive grabbed her shoulder. She flinched with such force the wine swung violently in her glass. She steadied it with both hands and set the goblet on the floor next to her.

"W-what?" Clive's greenish-blue gaze penetrated her soul… He never pitied her before. Her strong mind loathed pity. She could get herself out of any trouble, like today when she'd once again fought the informant. Then why now, as she stared into the incinerating logs, did she relate the leftover ashes to how quickly her time at S. F. Designs had come to an end? Yes, she wanted Clive to pity her. Because, she no longer believed she had it in her to fight. She would return to being a chef, and never once look back, because she'd never see the informant, or her company, again. But, is that what she wanted? To give up the company her father had dearly wished her to have?

Clive studied her with a hard look. "Mike followed the guy to his home in San Francisco. Trevor has his men watching the informant now."

Good. "Are they going to take him into custody?"

A muscle moved along Clive's jawline. "No," he said tightly. "We don't have evidence."

"What about the gun?"

His brow twitched. "We've got to keep watch and catch him in his next act."

Why had he skirted her question? "Next act? He pointed it *at me*." Only after she shouted the words, did she realize they weren't alone. The sudden silence around them alerted her that their friends had stopped what they were doing, and their attention narrowed at Clive and her.

"Eva." Clive's hand moved from her shoulder to her lower back, and with a gentle pull he drew her close to him.

She squeezed her eyes shut. *Dammit.* It wasn't a real gun. She knew that. She bit into her lower lip as though that could erase the past few minutes. Consumed by angst from the day's happenings, her mind had woven a story of its own. How did she forget the embarrassment? She'd handed the gun to Clive. He pulled the trigger. A tiny yellow flag with the word bang written in bright red shot out. No wonder the informant had sounded smug. She would too, if she got someone to believe that to be a real gun.

She exhaled. "Sorry. What am I saying?" Her feeble attempt to laugh did nothing to banish the worried look in Clive's expression. She glanced around the room. Nina sat on a reading chair next to the couch Carter and Marc were lounging on. Izzy and Allie sat at the dining table. Trevor leaned against a wall, his arms folded across his chest. They were staring. At her.

She drew in a shaky breath. "Sorry."

Clive placed a light kiss on her forehead and cuddled her tight against his chest, she sighed thankful that his embrace shielded her from the staring eyes.

"You know"—she cleared her throat—"it's good that he met me." She tilted her head backward and looked up at Clive. "At least now we know where he lives."

Clive nodded with her, but his eyes conveyed his distress.

"And—" She laughed without humor, kicking herself for not getting a grip on the situation already. "I don't know why I keep referring to it as a gun."

She tried hard to sound calm, but her blood boiled that the informant was still out there, free to scheme his next move. Real or not, he did point that thing at her, though only to warn her, but who's to say the next time he wouldn't be carrying a real weapon?

The laughter from those girls she'd heard right before she'd shouted for help rang in her ears. If only they'd taken the trail she'd been shoved on. If only she hadn't been preoccupied by memories of her family. If only she'd realized that she was skiing toward the wrong trail a few seconds before she had neared the edge. If only she hadn't lost her balance. If only she had shouted for help the moment she slipped off the cliff, maybe Clive would have heard her. If only…

"We're watching him round the clock, Eva." A dark frown had imprinted in Trevor's expression since finding about the new development with the informant.

She'd never seen him this annoyed.

"And when we don't meet his one-month deadline, he *will* make contact," Clive sounded as vengeful as Trevor looked.

"I can't wait to get my hands on that son of—" As though Trevor hadn't meant to display his aggravation in front of his girlfriend, he cut Nina a swift glance but then turned his head and stared at the fire, looking away from them all.

He will make contact. A piercing chill scurried down Eva's body. Her toes curled in her thick socks. Her skin raised into bumps.

Clive's embrace tightened around her and he rubbed down the length of her arms. His affection shooed her worries, but they darted right back. "We're not going to make his deadline?"

Clive eased his hold on her just enough to meet her gaze. "No. We're not." His slow tone, his questioning look, confirmed it hadn't struck him until now that she'd give in to the informant's threat. "It's *your* company, Eva. Your father wanted *you* to have it. And no one but *you* should be allowed to change that. You can't simply throw your life away because of another unfortunate encounter with that guy. And now that we know where he lives, and we also know that he has an accomplice who's calling the shots, no matter what they're up to next, we've got you covered." He moved his hands up to her shoulders and held her there. "We *will* get him this time. Alive or dead. He'll *never* see you again. I *will not* let him."

The determination in Clive's declaration, the warmth of his voice, the strength in his confidence, should have been enough to give her the courage she yearned for, but it didn't.

Because, in all these months, the informant had always found a way to contact her, no matter how closely Clive and Trevor had watched out for her. And next time, she didn't have a good feeling about the next time because something told her the informant would not carry a fake gun. Which meant danger for all of them. She darted her gaze again from Clive to Trevor to Carter to Nina to Izzy to Allie to Marc. She would never forgive herself if anything happened to any of her friends—and what about her mother? Her brother? And Clive's family? And all those who worked at S. F. Designs? She held back a gasp. What if the informant walked into her office, armed?

Defeated, she stared into the fireplace. As though to mimic her mood, the fire, too, quelled its glow and began simmering down. Numbed by her bleak thoughts, only as Clive shoved more logs into the fireplace, she realized he'd left her side.

Unbeaten, her worry meandered on to listing other people in her life who meant a great deal to her. Her Uncle Dave, Tina, the best secretary ever, and Tom. *Tom*. The way the informant mentioned his name she couldn't tell whether he feared him or disliked him, but for certain, he wouldn't hesitate to hurt Tom.

She never spent time alone anymore. On any given day, at least one or most of the people who were dear to her, were around her at all times. She closed her eyes tight and exhaled a shaky breath. She couldn't let him harm them. She wouldn't let him harm them.

"Eva." Allie crept close. "Just so you know, *this* is what a real gun looks like."

Eva stared in horror at the firearm Allie held flat in her palm.

"Give me that!" Trevor snatched the weapon away from Allie.

"Hey! I was only looking at it," Allie whined.

"Well, go look at it somewhere else." Trevor glowered at her long enough, then turned around and stormed away.

"I know a thing or two about guns, you know?" Allie followed Trevor.

He snapped his gun back into its holster. "Yeah? How's that?" he asked with as much bite as his glower.

Allie remained unfazed and popped onto the table to sit. "My father took me hunting sometimes. He has a small collection of guns. And speaking of, you should learn to use a firearm, Eva."

"Or at least know what one looks like." Izzy smirked at Allie. Allie snickered right back.

Eva wasn't just going to sit there and take their mockery. "First of all, that thing he pointed at me looked very real." Clive would agree. She turned her head and gave him a look that clearly demanded he back her up.

34

He stared. He blinked. He stared some more. "Y-you want me to agree."

The look she gave him now, though he continued to remain by her side, she could swear he would much prefer scooting as far away from her as possible. *Good.*

He cleared his throat. "Real." He nodded. "That gun looks very real."

She rolled her eyes and stood up. "And second of all, I'm not carrying a gun."

"Allie does make a good point, though," Marc added.

"She does not." Eva cut her gaze to Clive. "I'm *not* carrying a gun."

"How about this one?" Izzy turned her laptop around for them to view the screen.

Allie gasped. "No way. You can buy a gun online?"

Izzy narrowed her eyes. "A Pez dispenser, you dumb-dumb."

"What's Pez?"

Izzy gave Allie a strange look. "How have you never eaten Pez, the candy?"

"Bad parenting."

"Wait, didn't you go to the dentist a lot when we were growing up?"

"Oh, my God." Allie tilted her head back and groaned to the ceiling. "All the time. You remember when…"

Grateful their conversation had taken a diversion

from her, Eva went back to staring at the fire, and she downed the remainder of her wine.

Clive returned to her side. "You'll never see him again."

"What about that note he said I'll receive?"

"If he hand delivers it like he did all the times before, since we'll be following him everywhere he goes, we'll catch him in the act. You will not see him again."

She wouldn't argue. The seriousness in his tone along with his pained expression just went to show how much Clive loved her, and worried for her. She hoped he knew she wouldn't expect any less of him now that the informant had stepped up his game.

Trevor followed Clive. "*Never.*" His affirmation added to her feeble, but growing, confidence.

She looked around the room. The rest of the gang had silenced again and were back to staring at her. She had to ease the tension. "I'm so sorry, you guys. I owe you a vacation. We've got to rewrite this one."

"And I can help with that." Carter circled an arm around her shoulder and tugged her close in a friendly way. He refilled her glass with more burgundy.

"How about Santa Barbara? I'll give you all a tour of my winery and, of course, Clive can arrange something for you ladies at the spa."

"Sounds fun." It took little for Izzy and Allie to follow her lead and move on from the dreariness that loomed in everyone's minds.

For the first time since she'd met the informant

today, Eva smiled a genuine smile.

Clive brought his hand to her face and moved a few strands of stray hair to rest behind her ear. "Your smile, nothing compares to it." He kissed her lips. She kissed back.

Chapter 4

He'd eaten his usual microwavable dinner, watched his usual late-night TV, drank his usual beer, and yet the first night in his mother's house brought back the scariest of his childhood memories. He couldn't stay there another minute, let alone another day.

Every room had an association. Living room, where his father slept most nights. Kitchen, where his mother flung dishes at his father while they argued. Bathtub, where his father tried to slit his wrists once. But he survived. *His biggest failure*, his mother mocked.

His childhood bedroom remained his only solace. Though momentary, being in that room brought him relief when he rummaged through a cardboard box filled with his school day favorites. His books, his pirate ship, his red car, one of his milk teeth... Which one of his teeth was it?

But his nostalgia remained short lived as the voices of his parents—shouting, fighting—reverberated in his mind. Despite living with his parents, his family, his childhood days were the loneliest days he'd ever lived.

He turned on the TV to its loudest, threw a pillow and a blanket below his childhood bed, and crawled under. The space was not big enough for an adult, and he bruised his knees and bumped his head as he crept against the cold tile floor. But that had been where he'd slept most of his teenage days. And today, more than ever before, sleeping there was better than sleeping on his bed. Because how could he forget that rare day that he dared to sleep in his bed and not under it, when his mother had shaken him awake. Dragged him into her bedroom.

"Watch. Learn."

He gripped the side of the doorframe and stared in horror as his father lay unmoving and bloodied on their bed. His father raised a red hand. "Billy," he'd asked, his voice hoarse as he reached to hold him one last time. Before he could react to his father's request, his mother raised a kitchen knife and stabbed his father in the chest over and over and over.

He wouldn't stay in this house another day. Tomorrow, he'd return to his boat. He didn't care about his employer's threats. *Fuck it. Fuck it all to hell.* That became his lullaby for the night, just to be able to sleep.

But morning light brought with it his lust for money. Spending the night there had been enough of a torture, but he convinced himself that he'd do it again. He wanted nothing more than to get paid. But, he wouldn't hang around there all day. He'd do anything to avoid reliving his past.

Chapter 5

After the weekend she'd had, determined to not let anything bring her down, Eva strode into her office ready for whatever the day would bring her way. She swung the door to her room open and stepped in with a carefree spring. Upon seeing her uncle standing by the bay window next to her desk, she came to an abrupt halt.

"Hey, you." *What's he doing here?* "Morning." *Please, let it be good news.*

He turned around to face her. "Hey yourself." The way he grinned, he wanted to tell her something positive.

Though somewhat skeptical about his optimism, given he did wait for her in her office instead of doing his usual and phone her, she let her worries simmer low until she heard him out.

"Did you have a good weekend?" He shoved his hands into his pants pockets and sauntered toward the couch.

"Mm-hmm." To avoid giving away her anxiety that had spiked right up from his harmless question, she turned to her side and looked away from him. She slipped off her jacket and hung it on the freestanding coat rack. She needed to switch to a less unnerving topic. "We're going to Santa Barbara one of these weekends. Do some wine tasting, visit the spa. Should be fun."

She tried to sound unruffled, but her insides tumbled from anticipating being probed about the past weekend. Every detail of her encounter with the informant played in front of her eyes.

Happy thoughts, her subconscious mind instructed.

Yes. She cleared her throat. No more negativity. *Only happy thoughts.* She dragged in a deep breath and faced her uncle, hoping he hadn't caught her evasion.

"Ah, that spa."

Though she should feel victorious for dodging that one, and though her workday full of meetings had yet to begin, her shoulders already felt heavy, her body already hurt, and her energy had drained from being reminded of her encounter with the informant.

She brought a hand to her neck and massaged the tightness. She should have taken the day off. She should have taken the week off. She should have snuggled into her couch with a good book, or a movie, or Clive. *Clive...* And just like that, her anxiety converted to happiness, to hope, to love. Thoughts of Clive always brought her to a certain high, because how could they not? Her heart warmed, her body loosened. She gained the calm she needed to find out why her uncle was visiting at the start of her day.

"It was our first big project," he said. "How we loved designing that spa. And then that feeling of accomplishment once we were done, it was something else." He relaxed on the couch.

She didn't remember when she'd seen her uncle this casual. He rested one hand in his lap and let the other hang over the back of the sofa. That grin still hadn't left his face. What did he want to tell her?

"You know, the night before we opened it to the public for the first time, the Stanfords, your parents, myself, and of course your aunt, just the six of us had a private celebration on that beach."

"Really?" She hadn't known that. "That must have been some night."

"I cannot remember a better celebration. We sat around a bonfire, gazed at the stars, drank, talked about our future. We stayed on the beach till dawn." His eyes downcast, he stared at the vintage wooden coffee table in front of him for a long moment. A light smile lingered on his face, as though he was visualizing that night, reliving it in that moment.

"How was your weekend?" Eva set her bag on her desk and settled into a chair opposite her uncle.

"The usual."

Before she could probe further, a slight knock on the door interrupted their conversation. Tina walked in. "Eva, hey."

Her secretary's eyes widened, just enough for Eva to suspect Tina knew why her uncle was visiting.

She raised her brows at Tina. *C'mon, spill.*

Tina held her gaze.

So?

Tina gave her a questioning look, and then turned toward her uncle.

"Here's your coffee, Mr. Avery. Milk and sugar on the side." The white porcelain coffee cup clinked against the saucer it rested on as Tina placed the metal tray on the low side table next to Uncle Dave. "Would you like anything else?"

"No, thank you. This is perfect. Nothing like the aroma of freshly brewed coffee."

"Right?" she added.

"Especially when *you* make it." He gave her a sweet smile. "Did I ever tell you, you make the best coffee?"

"Oh stop." She pushed at his shoulder and giggled.

"I mean it. But don't tell my wife I said that."

"Thank you, Mr. Avery." Tina gave him a wide grin and turned her attention to Eva. Her gaze fell to the take-out cup in Eva's hand. "You have enough tea? Do you need a refill?"

Only then did Eva realize how tightly she was holding the cup. Reminding herself to not let anything bring her down, she eased her grip. *Relax.* She slowed her exhale. "I'm good. Thanks."

Tina gave her a nod and left the room. The door clicked closed behind her.

Eva drew her attention back to her uncle. He picked up a sugar cube with a tiny pair of tongs, dropped it into his cup, and poured in milk.

"So, what's up?" She held her breath, eager to hear what had made her uncle so delighted today.

But just as she asked, his grin faded. Instead of answering her right away, he dipped a silver spoon into the cup and stirred. The coffee swirled, as did Eva's insides. She had no clue what he'd been about to say, but that he took his time to unveil his thoughts most likely meant it couldn't be a happy announcement.

She scooted to the edge of her seat to set her teacup on the table before she crushed it. She intertwined her fingers tightly, digging her nails into the backs of her hands, a move she'd picked up after taking over her father's company to help distract her from the constant mental pain. Maybe the informant's idea that she should leave her company would be to her benefit after all. She should seriously consider it.

He sipped his coffee. "Really. Best coffee ever. I'll miss this."

Miss this? That's when it hit her.

"No," she mumbled. She shook her head. "No."

She sprang from her seat and rushed off toward her desk. To do what exactly? She didn't know. But her breath raced, her chest hurt, tears rushed to her eyes. "You're leaving me." She faced him, willing him to tell her she'd gotten it all wrong. But he didn't.

"Yes."

"Why?" She raced back to her chair and perched on the cushion.

"Because, it's time."

"Time for what?"

"For me to step out of your limelight."

My limelight? Our limelight. "But how am I…" *supposed to make decisions here without you?* "How will I…" *handle the board, the clients, the employees?* "What if…" *I fail?*

"Eva." He laughed. "Are you serious right now? How do you not see that you're handling the company better than I ever could? You don't need me here. Your father would be proud of you. *I'm* proud of you. Besides, I've kept my promise to your father and now my job is done."

"No. It's not. I need you here."

"You don't. You're the one making everything around here happen. For the past few months, I've been on the sidelines, watching your every move. People love you here, they respect you, and they'll do anything for you. You've achieved it all by yourself. You've turned a failing company to profit again. Don't ever forget that achievement. It's yours. It's all yours to feel great about."

Maybe so, but she only got to where she was

because of him being with her at every step. His leaving meant she'd no longer have her shield, her pillar of strength, her fallback plan, her uncle.

Brokenhearted and unable to conjure any words that would help her convince him to stay, she cried. Heavy tears sprinted down her face.

He stretched his arm toward her and held her hand in his. His skin warm. Hers cold. "I'm always only a phone call away."

She nodded, but the tears kept rolling. She reached for a tissue from a dispenser on the table and dabbed her face.

What had happened to her? She never cried like this in public, and never in front of her uncle. The weekend's happenings had already set a heavy burden on her, and now... *You are stronger than this. Happy thoughts, remember?* She brought another tissue to her eyes and blotted.

"I've gone through a lot since your father's passing, Eva. We all have." He exhaled and shifted deeper into his seat. "But you're still young. And I'm...I'm tired, you know? I'm ready for retirement."

Yes, he'd been through a lot. Added to the shock of her father's passing, her uncle had helped hold the company up through the initial difficult months. It had only gotten worse for him when the FBI began hounding him about his involvement in her father's death. His loyalty in question, the board members nearly ousted him from the company.

He deserved none of that. Yet he'd dealt with it

all, only for Eva's sake, to help her get to where she should be, to help her live up to the legacy her father had left behind, to ensure she'd become comfortable with handling the company by herself.

Initially, the board had disapproved of her every action. She fought her fights. She won some; she lost many. At the end of the day, she shrugged it all off. Just like she should now. Her uncle no longer wanted to work at her company. She should allow him that freedom. Besides, with the threat from the informant rising, regardless of Clive and Trevor's plan to deal with him, if she were to leave in a month's time, the less involvement her uncle had in S. F. Designs, the better.

She nodded as though agreeing with her own thoughts.

"How long would you like to stay?"

"Well, like I said, you've been handling the business very well and there's nothing else left to hand over to you. So, one month?"

One month...what's up with that timeline nowadays?

Her uncle gave her a questioning look. She managed a light smile and dabbed the last of the wetness from her face. "What are you going to do?"

"Honestly"—he raised his brows—"I don't know." He laughed. "Sleep in. Play golf. Read a nonbusiness book." He half shrugged and laughed some more. "I simply don't know." He looked happy, which lightened some of the heaviness in her heart. "But first, I've got to find out how my morning coffee would taste spiked."

***

Her day passed in recollecting every memory she'd shared with her uncle. The many times they'd waited in the coffee shop for her father to get done with his meetings. The many times they'd played card games at her grandpa's house, her uncle always helping her win. The many times he'd visited her brother and her in their boarding school to sneak them away. *I'll buy you however much ice cream you want.* The many times he'd helped recover from her mistakes when she had started to work at her father's company. Together, they'd repaired the company, built it into a business different from the one her father had owned, one that showcased Eva's ideas and ideals.

And before she knew it, the one person she'd always depended on to give her that ray of hope when she needed it the most had decided to leave her to her fate. Why had it never occurred to her that this day would be inevitable? Why had she never imagined managing her company without her uncle?

Her phone tinkling jolted her back from her musing. *Clive. What time is it?* She peeked at her wristwatch. *It's five already?* She reached for her phone. *Not Clive.* Her mother's picture appeared on the screen.

"Hey, Mom." She tried to sound as cheerful as she could.

"Evie, you sound terrible. Is everything okay?"

Her mother's intuition, ever vigilant, brought Eva a smile. Because whether in person, over the phone, in an email, or in a text message, her mother always got Eva's temperament right.

Although tempted to tell her everything, the way Eva's past few days had gone, it would take a whole weekend with her mother to even begin to make her understand the downward spiral her life had taken. In her childhood home, gorging on the world's best macaroni and cheese only her mother could make, and of course, drinking countless glasses of red wine… Should she call it a weekend already?

She sighed to herself. Because while she would like nothing better than to reveal every detail of what had been plaguing her since she'd taken over from her father, any hint about the present situation with the informant would only make her mother worry for her more.

"I'm fine." She leaned her chair as far back as it would go. She stayed at that angle and stared at the white ceiling.

"No, you're not. And I understand if you just tell me you don't want to talk about it right now. But what I will not take from you, Eva, is a lie."

Eva sighed, aloud this time, and rubbed one of her eyes with the back of her finger. Her eye burned. "You're right. I don't want to talk about it right now."

"Good. And I'll remember to ask you in a few days."

"Thanks, Mom. And, sorry about the lie."

"Oh, honey, it's okay. Don't worry about it. I'm sure you have good reason for whatever it is you're keeping to yourself. And I'm sorry you aren't happy, and maybe…" A slight laugh in her mother's tone confirmed her mood had lightened. "I know the exact thing to cheer you up."

"Yeah?"

"Yep. Guess?"

Her mother's happiness contagious, Eva laughed along with her. She leaned toward her desk, set her elbow on it, and rested her chin on her palm. "Okay. Joey's back."

"Nope."

"No?"

"No."

"Huh." She drummed her fingertips against the side of her face. "Then…ah…"

"C'mon. This one's easy."

That didn't sound like her mother. "Diane?" She didn't know her mother was meeting Clive's mother today. "Am I on speaker? Where are you both?"

"On speaker, yes. Where? At home. And you are obviously wondering what we are up to."

Not anymore, because their giggles meant only one thing.

"We're discussing your wedding," her mother announced.

Of course, they were. Eva slid her face down and rested one side of her forehead on her palm. She'd walked right into their trap, unprepared for what had now become their usual drama.

"Because someone's got to, seeing how neither you nor Clive are. Can you tell us why that is?" Diane asked.

And that's how it always started. *Dammit. I had something for this.* She'd planned for the exact conversation. She'd practiced a rebuttal. If only she could remember what she had intended to say. She flipped through the Post-it notes on her desk. She could swear she'd written it somewhere. "I'm sorry, I don't understand." That should buy her time.

"It's been four months since you got engaged. When are you going to start planning your wedding?"

"Y-yeah, we haven't got there yet." She flipped through the pages of her notepad. She tugged her desk drawer. It didn't open. She tugged it again. It remained jammed. She tapped her phone screen, put the call on speaker, and set her mobile on her desk. She held the knob on the drawer with both hands and yanked it so hard the drawer flew right out. Though it fell on the carpet, it met the floor with a loud thud.

"What's that?" Diane asked.

"Ah, nothing. Just a a sorry. What were we talking about, again?"

"See, this is what she does." Her mother caught on. "Every time I bring up her wedding, this is *exactly* how she evades." Her tone exaggerated her irritation.

"I'm not evading." Eva tried hard not to shout,

given the many times she'd had this same conversation with her mother. This time, she blamed her mother for making her a liar. Yes, Eva had evaded this interrogation for months now, and so had Clive. They were enjoying the *fiancé thing* they had going. Hanging out with friends. Going out on dates. And, of course, the sex was terrific. Like this morning. Her heart skittered a beat as that visual flashed into her mind. Despite their best intentions to get ready in time for work, they'd showed up late. They'd made out before their shower. They'd made out after their shower. Never tried to do it in the shower, though.

"Oh, you're not doing that?"

"No, we haven't. But—" Wait. What? How did they get to talking about her sex life? She stilled. Had she spoken about shower sex aloud? She scrunched her eyes shut and cleared her throat. "I-I don't feel comfortable talking about this."

"See? What did I say? Always evading," her mother complained.

"What?" Eva shook her head fast hoping that would help return her thoughts to the conversation blaring through her phone.

"What do you mean, *what*?"

She stared at the drawer on the floor, some of its contents fallen out. She'd fix it later. She had her crazy mother, and crazier future mother-in-law, to worry about. "Can you be more specific?"

"*When's* your wedding date? *Where* is your wedding? How many people will you be inviting?

Did you prepare the invitation? What flavor is your cake?"

She leaned back into her chair and stared at the ceiling. "Mother, I get it. But—"

"And her dress—" Diane added.

Clink.

Clink? Of course, they were drinking. And rejoicing at her dismay. Eva mentally groaned. Unless she somehow disrupted this conversation, there would be no going home tonight.

"Right. *Your* dress," her mother chimed in.

"And Clive's tux," Diane said.

"And the tux. Right." They clinked again.

"And what's everyone else going to wear?"

"Exactly!"

No point in explaining once again to her mother, or Diane, that neither Clive nor she cared about getting married the traditional way. Had their mothers not whined and wailed, dissing their suggestion to keep their wedding simple, a private affair, they would have been married already. They would have had a lavish after-party with their friends and family. Heck, they might be on their honeymoon right now. The informant would not have threatened her. Her uncle wouldn't have resigned. And most of all, she and Clive wouldn't have to endure this cyclic wedding-planning intervention. But as luck would have it, their mothers had an agenda of their own. One that involved a lot of work, which again, neither Clive nor she cared for.

Eva angled her elbow on the armrest of her chair, rested her chin on her palm, and let her gaze dip to the fallen cabinet. *Oh, there you are.* She leaned toward the floor and picked up a box of chocolate truffles from the drawer. She forgot she'd hidden them away from Izzy and Allie's prying eyes. Because, while she would savor a truffle slowly, and try to detect the ingredients, which she'd then tally with the description chart that came with the chocolates, her friends would have emptied the rest of the box. *Savages.*

Given the weight of the box, her friends had not found its hiding place. She smirked at her success, opened the tin lid, and…*the Post-it.* Oh right, she'd left it in there because she suspected she'd reach for the chocolates when she talked to her mother.

"Are you even listening to us, Eva?"

"Sure."

Letting her mother and Diane rant on, Eva plopped a cocoa-coated ball into her mouth. Mmm, medium-dark chocolate ganache with a pinch of cayenne. She closed her eyes. The words blaring from her phone had lost all coherence as the flavors melted in her mouth. *Yep, that's it.* She opened the description chart. Ganache. Good. Cayenne. Of course. She gave herself a mental high-five. How she loved being smug about anything related to cooking. But wait. She reread the last ingredient. Coconut? Had she tasted coconut? She gulped the last of the chocolate. *Coconut? Really?* The description had to be wrong. She read it again. Maybe she hadn't concentrated with all the chatter growing louder and louder from her phone. Or maybe her skills were weakening? Since she'd taken over the company, she had little to no time to cook. But seriously, though, that couldn't happen. She couldn't lose her culinary skills. Could she?

"What do *you* think?" Diane asked.

"I don't think that can happen."

"What? Why not?" Diane snapped.

Shit. The wedding. Not her ingredient detecting skills. "You know what…" Eva picked up the Post-it and scanned through the one and only bullet point. *Let them do it.*

Oh yeah, Clive and she had reached that decision the night Izzy and Carter invited them over for dinner, a surprise bachelor-bachelorette party. Other than her friends shouting surprise when she and Clive had entered Izzy's house, then downing a few of those special drinks Izzy's hired bartender had mixed for the would-be bride and groom, Eva remembered nothing else from that night.

"We know what, Eva? Are you ever telling us, or are you evading, *again*?"

She cleared her throat. "You both have really awesome ideas. I mean, Clive and I would be honored if you'd be willing to take over all the planning for our wedding."

Diane gasped. "No way."

No way as in, *no way they're letting us do this*, or *no way we're doing all that work*?

"Really?" The delight in her mother's tone resolved Eva's confusion.

"Absolutely." She'd never expected them to be so thrilled by the prospect of planning their wedding. To think of it now, had she and Clive known any better, they would have handed the reins over to their mothers months ago. "You have a dream wedding in mind, and Clive has offered to spare no cost, so yeah, really, let's make that happen." She plopped another one of those truffles into her mouth.

"No. No. That won't do."

"I'm with Diane on this. We're paying for it, Eva. Diane and I. Together. That's our condition if you want us to plan your wedding."

Oh great. They were back to the who-pays-for-the-wedding discussion. Again. "Clive will not agree to that."

"You don't worry about that. Francis will handle Clive," Diane assured.

Well, if Eva knew one thing about Clive, he could negotiate a way out of any compromise. "Okay." She half shrugged.

"Yeah? Then we're in."

"Yay!" They clinked their glasses again. "Now, here's what we've got to do first…"

While Diane laid out a plan, Eva drifted away. W*hite chocolate with—what's that? Mmm, I know this. What* is *it?* She'd eaten the entire truffle but couldn't name the mystery ingredient she'd tasted.

She shouldn't look at the description.

Yet she slanted her eyes toward the leaflet. The words blurred from that angle.

Unable to trust herself, she turned the pamphlet over, blank side up.

It is...

Dammit. What is it? She flipped the paper over and hurriedly read the ingredients that had gone into that truffle.

Oh, persimmon. Of course, I know that. How hadn't she guessed it? She had the fruit tree in her backyard, after all. Sadness drowned her heart. Her skills were definitely diminishing and working at S. F. Designs would only make it worse. And now that her uncle had decided to leave too, she'd never be able to open that restaurant of her dreams. "This is terrible," she mumbled.

"What do you mean?" Her mother's miffed tone dragged Eva back into their wedding planning.

She squeezed her eyes shut in pure annoyance with herself, how had she once again spoken her thoughts aloud.

"*You* said we could plan your wedding, and *this is* our plan, Eva."

Eva kicked herself for having sounded ungrateful.

"And *why* exactly is it *terrible*?" Diane's tone matched her mother's.

Arg. Eva loved her mother. She loved Diane. She loved how much happiness planning her wedding brought them. She also loved chocolate. She cut a look to the tin box and nearly reached to pick out another truffle.

Chapter 6

No amount of truffles could cure the hole the news about her uncle leaving the company had bored through her heart. Eva stared at the darkness the lack of light had cast on the otherwise white ceiling. Clive slept next to her, on his stomach, snoring lightly—his signature position. Any other night, she could stare at him for hours, recollecting all the memories she'd created with him, all the times they grew a little closer than they had before. But tonight, her thoughts remained consumed by the memories she'd shared with her uncle and the irreplaceable emptiness he'd already begun to leave behind.

She turned on her side, facing away from Clive, and reached for her cell phone she'd set on the bedside table. She brought the phone under the quilt to shield its glow from waking Clive. She tapped on its screen. *Argh. Only one fifteen.* Five hours and forty-five minutes more before her alarm would go off. She should really try to hush her thoughts and get at least a few more hours of sleep.

She abandoned her phone on the table and turned to face Clive. Her otherwise passionate, sensual lover slept calm and peaceful. She smiled thinking of him that way and closed her eyelids as though not allowing the image to escape. They stung from lack of sleep. She shut them tight to dissipate the burn, and it helped, but only for a long minute because she just couldn't keep them closed. She couldn't sleep. She turned to her back, and this time Clive moved around and faced away from her. She remained still till his exhales once again ended in a light snore. With small movements she slid out of the bed, tiptoed out of the room, and closed the door behind her.

Curled to one side of the couch, she pulled a velvet throw over her, took the remote off the coffee table, switched the TV on, and flipped through the channels.

Guy selling an indestructible pan. *Next.*

Woman selling makeup. *Next.*

Guy selling a dishtowel that soaks up almost anything. *Next.*

Celebrity Poker. *Next.*

Horror movie. Next. Next. Next. Reflecting on her own life, why would anyone *want to* get scared?

And, *off.*

She tossed the remote to her side, and it bounced to one corner of the couch.

She strolled to the window. Fog had covered the

entire cityscape. Only a few lights glimmered from within. Perfect weather to snuggle into the couch and read a good book.

She strolled to Clive's study. One of the walls, a floor to ceiling window, remained blanketed by the fog. Another, all glass, faced the living room. The remaining two were floor to ceiling bookshelves. Clive had really great taste in books. She perused the shelves, and found many of her favorites that she had read numerous times and many that she'd always wanted to read. She pulled out one of the books.

One of these weekends she should hide out in this reading chair, as she did now, and read all day, and do nothing much else.

She rested her legs on the ottoman, covered herself with the velvet throw she'd brought from the living room, flipped open the book, raised it to her nose, and took a deep breath. The familiar fragrance of paper returned memories from her childhood, of the many summer afternoons she'd spent reading her favorite stories. She'd sit in her grandpa's rocking chair on the patio overlooking the vineyards and read for hours. Like Clive, her grandpa had an impressive home library.

She read through the first page and couldn't ignore how bad her eyes stung each time she blinked. But sleep had abandoned her. She continued to read. Fiction, her go-to genre, she read the first chapter, then the next, and she went on until her body craved a stretch. She pushed her legs as far out as she could and pointed her toes, when her gaze cut to an antique clock embedded into one of the shelves. *Really?*

She'd read for two hours straight.

She yawned and closed her eyes. They stung worse than they ever did. She hated to part from the book, but she should really get some sleep. She brought a finger to the corner of her eye and wiped a small tear. *One eighty-four*, the number of the page she'd last read. She shut the book and set it on the side table.

She strolled to the kitchen and poured herself a glass of water, and her gaze drifted to the liquor cabinet. Maybe she should drink something stronger? And regret her decision in the morning when she'd have to head to work with a full-blown hangover? Tempting. *But, water it is.*

Back in the living space, she looked around the room, not sure what to do next, and her gaze fell to an almost invisible indentation in the wall. She walked toward the panel, and it slid open without making the slightest noise. Her heart almost jumped out of her chest at the surprise of the hidden door.

Lights turned on, revealing a flight of stairs heading upward to a secret floor. How had she never seen this before?

A cool breeze brushed past her. She tightened her robe and ascended the stairs. She reached the top and came to an abrupt halt, in awe at the rooftop garden that spanned the entire length of Clive's apartment. Bamboo trees, flowering bushes, and a lush lawn covered the pathway she followed. When the greenery cleared somewhat, she stepped with caution onto the pebbled floor, and her gaze stuck at a pristine blue pool that spanned ahead of her. Light steam rolled up from the water and vanished the instant it met the cold breeze.

Like everything Clive owned, this space seemed to have come to life right out of a luxury outdoor design catalogue. Who'd have imagined one of the busiest neighborhoods of downtown San Francisco would host a garden such as this serene, tranquil, mid-city escape.

One moment, the ambience gave her the exact detachment she needed from her crazy day, but in the next, her darkest fear shadowed it all.

Water, lots of water—lots of deep water. The more she gazed at the pool, the larger and deeper it got. Her skin awoke, her hair raised, not from the lingering breeze and the cold fog sweeping around her, but from the images of her drowning incident flashing through her mind. That moment when her strength had failed, the moment when she had begun sinking, the moment when she saw the blue of the sky rippling away, that moment in the lake by her grandpa's house.

Like she had been that day, she was frantic for breath now, and she took a quick step back. She almost shrieked when she bumped into…"Clive." She exhaled.

The glow from the dim lights hidden behind the bushes deepened the darkness of his mood. His jaw clenched, his eyes filled with a mix of anger and curiosity, the way he stood, with his hands tucked into his joggers, he'd been there all this time, watching her. One moment, they studied each other. The next, he circled his arms around her and pulled her to his chest. Radiating warmth from his hug soothed her frazzled nerves.

"You never told me." She hadn't meant to whine, but she sort of did, because all this time she'd lived under this enormous, gigantic ocean of water not knowing that she did. "It's—" She licked her lips. "It's huge." Even as she said it, her muscles grew stiffer.

"Not the first time you've said that."

She pulled back and glared at him.

He grinned, a hot grin. Really? An innuendo? In that moment, at her plight? "Not funny, Clive." She pushed his chest with both hands, but he did not budge. Instead, he tightened his hold on her.

Humor vanished from his features. "It's four feet deep at that halfway mark. Deepest is that end. Only six feet."

She didn't want to look.

"Eva…"

She sighed at the honeyed persuasion in his tone. She cut her gaze to where he pointed with one finger but turned her head right back into his chest. "Only? Only six feet?"

He placed a light kiss to her forehead. "You know how to swim."

"I know how to drown." *He knew that.*

"I can teach you how not to."

His effortless comforting should have eased any and all of her worries, yet she shivered tensely. He cocooned her closer.

They stayed like that for the longest second, and then he asked, "Wanna try?"

No. She pressed her ear against his chest and remained there.

"C'mon. We'll be quick."

She pressed herself into him more.

He kissed her forehead again, and she looked up at him.

"You mean now?"

He grinned that grin, again, that hypnotized almost anyone to do exactly what he wanted, but she willed hard for it to not work on her this time.

"It's nearly four in the morning, Clive." She took a step back, and he stepped with her, keeping her locked within his arms, as though they were dancing. She took another step back, and he followed her again. Which had been cute, but she gave him her best stern look. "Are you serious right now?"

"Yep. You're not sleepy, and neither am I. So why don't we get in from that shallow end, right there, which is only three feet, by the way. Relax in the warm water for a bit, and…that's all."

"Relax?"

He kissed her lips this time. "Yes. Please relax." He kissed the tip of her nose. His actions eased her plenty, but his words made her a nervous wreck.

She gazed worriedly at the shallow end where he'd suggested they should *relax*, but then she found just the escape. "How about that Jacuzzi? Let's relax there." Now she grinned a pretty-please grin, which from her past experience guaranteed to get him to do exactly what she wanted.

"Sure. Let's. *After* we relax there first." He jerked his chin toward the pool.

But she wouldn't give in that easy. "I don't have a swimsuit." Score!

"I bought you one."

"What? When?"

"A while back. I bought you a couple different styles, actually. Wasn't sure which one you'd like."

Her shoulders got heavy. Her body tightened. She exhaled hard. She'd run out of excuses to avoid his plan.

He cupped his warm hand behind her head and massaged the sides of her neck. That felt *so* good.

Until once again, she cut her gaze to the shallow end. She could swear it looked a lot deeper than three feet.

She exhaled another heavy breath. How did she always get herself into situations like this?

Had she stayed in bed, tossing, turning, uncomfortable and unable to sleep, she wouldn't be in this mess right now. Had she continued to flip those TV channels, maybe for a change chosen to watch that scary movie, which she otherwise would never dare to watch, she wouldn't be in this mess right now. Had she poured that big glass of wine and returned to reading, she wouldn't be in this mess right now. Had she done anything, just about anything, besides taking those idiot stairs to this idiot terrace, she wouldn't be in this mess right now.

Regardless of all the terrible choices she'd made in the last half hour, if she'd told Clive, only once, that she didn't want to get into that water, he wouldn't force her to do anything she didn't want to do, and she wouldn't be in this mess right now.

Though she resisted acting on his suggestion, why didn't she tell him she didn't want to swim?

Maybe because, after all that destiny had thrown her way, her parents separating, her father's passing, the failing company she had inherited, her uncle leaving, the informant—especially the informant—she hated that she could do nothing about the one-month deadline he'd imposed. Taking up Clive's challenge, in a way, helped her to believe in her strengths again. With Clive by her side, she could overcome the unthinkable, but to be able to swim again? It would take lot of determination to sway her protesting mind. Just as much strength as it would take her to stand against the informant's threat. Or even lead the company without her uncle for that matter. And the only way to accomplish any of those would be for her to at least try.

She forced herself to turn around and face the pool. From behind, Clive tugged her to him once more. They stood like that, as though waiting for her to make the next move, as though Clive understood she needed to prepare her mind, her heart, for the leap of courage she was about to take.

He placed a light kiss at that vulnerable spot on her neck. "I'll hold you just like this through it all. I promise."

Her skin tingled into bumps again, but this time,

from the warmth of Clive's touch, from the hoarseness of his deep voice, from how he tended to her every worry, her every like, her every dislike.

"I'll never let go." He kissed her neck again. "I promise."

***

Fourteen years since she'd worn a swimsuit. This would be the first time she'd ever worn an adult version of it. From the ones Clive had bought for her, she picked a white one-piece, leaving the bikini for a more daring day.

All that courage she'd mustered earlier dissipated the moment she neared the pool again. Clive got to it first. The water reached up to his upper thighs, an indicator for her as to the depth she would step into. He extended a hand for her to take, but she remained still, unable to blink away from the vast overwhelming water.

"Ready?"

One moment she was biting her lower lip and rooted to the tiled ledge, and the next, Clive grabbed her waist and lowered her into the warm water.

She shrieked.

"Breathe." He laughed.

She licked her lips and managed a light smile.

He held her hand and walked her deeper into the pool, and she followed until the water rose hip deep. She had no clue why or how, but she lowered to her knees, letting the water submerge her to her shoulders.

Clive joined her there.

Her gaze hovered to the deep end of the pool until Clive brushed his lips against hers. The look in his eyes as he slipped her hair behind her ear showed how much he worried for her, how much he loved her. He traced her jaw with his finger, relaxing her enough to unclench her teeth and loosen her grip on his arm. She let go only slightly, and her fingers had imprinted his biceps. She rubbed his skin to soothe.

"You know, per the original blueprint of this building, this should have been a tennis court."

"Really? Good that it isn't, because it's beautiful here." The scattered fog, the trees, the gazebo, and the warm water that had begun easing her tightened nerves took her far from reality. Reality, which if she were to pay attention, would have caused her to have a panic attack and run as far away as possible from this enormous pool, from Clive's apartment, maybe even from the building.

"It is."

"So, why the change?"

"Emma."

"Your niece?"

"Yep. She wanted a swimming pool for her birthday. Her mother wouldn't let her have one, so her uncle did."

"She swims?"

"She thinks she does." He chuckled. "I set up a

net behind there"—he tilted his head over his shoulder to indicate the spot—"so she won't float over to the deeper end."

He told her where he'd set the net. He pressed on the possibility of keeping the barrier there, permanently, for Emma, of course. Though he didn't say it to her in as many words, he planted the idea in her mind that he'd make her feel as safe as possible if she ever wanted to try out the pool by herself.

"Thanks."

He smiled back, not asking her what she'd thanked him for. He kissed her lips one more time, and then gazed at the far end of the pool.

"Emma." He let out a light laugh. A smile lingered on his face. Cute how happy he looked in that moment, an otherwise influential and authoritative businessman, taking pride in catering to every whim of a three-year-old.

"Stop staring at me," he mumbled, but smiled some more.

"Make me."

He splashed water at her. She splashed back at him. They took a few more turns until he caught her hand and pulled her to him for a long, consuming, addictive kiss. Why had she ever hesitated to get into the pool with Clive?

"Wanna swim?"

Oh, that's why. She shook her head.

He didn't ask her a second time. He didn't say anything else either.

"But you should," she pressed.

The seriousness in his expression hit deep in her chest. "I'm not leaving you here by yourself."

Her sweet, sweet Clive. She couldn't say she was ready to be left by herself in the pool, given how close her anxiety attack lurked, waiting for the slightest opportunity to pounce. But she couldn't tie Clive down because of her irrational fear either. "I'm fine," she cajoled, kissing his cheek. "Go. Please."

His brows pulled closer, and his gaze bore into hers.

"Yes. I'm sure. Go on." She placed her palm flat on his chest and pushed him away from her. The motion did nothing to sway him, but she moved to a sidewall, losing all bodily contact with Clive. Only then did it hit her, for the first time since she'd entered the pool, she wasn't clutching Clive's arm for life. Willingly. *Progress.*

As though the same thought ran in his mind, he grinned. "Something very sexy about brave women."

"Yeah? How many sexy brave women do you know?"

"Only one."

"Are you going to reward me then?"

"Oh, you thought I was speaking about you?"

She splashed water at him. He turned his head, avoiding the splatter. She splashed him again, with both hands this time. Before she knew it, he caught both her wrists and tugged her to him. He picked her up and set her on the heated ledge of the pool. He set his hands flat on the floor next to her, and his biceps flexed as he pulled himself up in one quick move. Water splashed away from his body and created an enormous ripple where he'd once stood. Had she really thought he'd swim away, leaving her grasping for her life? His show of affection let loose a sparkle of longing from her chest to the tips of her toes. Her muscles tightened, her core clenched, her toes curled, as though that could hold on to the amazing sensation a little longer.

Though he'd asked her into the pool and pulled her into the water before she could muster strength to step in herself, once they were in, he'd let her lead. They stayed in the shallow end however long she wanted, no questions asked. They'd moved in deeper only when she wanted to, no questions asked. Not once had he let her feel ashamed of her vulnerability, which left her with a renewed determination to overcome her fear once and for all. Being able to swim again seemed more achievable than anything else that had been going on in her life. And she had Clive to thank for that nudge of confidence.

Tall and strong, he stood before her, and her head fell back as she gazed the length of the elegant man who'd become her world. Whether he dressed casually, or in one of his luxurious suits, whether he bared it all, or wore simple navy swim trunks, just being in his presence could become an addiction. Whether in public, or with their work colleagues, or even their friends, she noticed people didn't just glance at Clive. Their gazes lingered on him. Being good looking was one thing, but Clive exuded more than mere looks. His charming personality, mixed with a gentle yet powerful ability to control everything and everybody, hypnotized the world to gravitate to him, like she did now.

She loved this man. And he loved her. How had she ever lived without him? Did he ever think of her that way? Could she ever mean as much to him as he did to her?

He strode toward a basket and pulled out a white towel. He paced back to her, wrapped her in it, and before she could do or say anything, towel and all, he carried her to the Jacuzzi.

Before they got there, she whispered, "Let's skip it."

***

The depth in her words hit him so fast his breath seized in his chest. The longing tenderness in her eyes spoke of more passion than her words. Yes, he wanted her just as bad.

He brought them within a circle of bamboo trees, set her down to stand, and tossed their towels into a nearby basket. Automatic sensors unleashed heated pearls of water to rain on them from the overhead outdoor shower.

Her skin glistened from the light reflecting off the droplets that skittered off her shoulders.

"Now, what exactly did you want to skip? This?" He kissed the side of her neck as he peeled off one strap of her swimsuit. "Or this?" He slid the other strap off, kissing her collarbone as he went.

Trapped within his arms with nowhere to go, she leaned her head back and looked at him. He envied the wet beads that trickled down her delicate features, touching her everywhere before he did.

She pushed down his shorts, and he kicked them away.

Her hands roamed all over him. He loved how her fingertips danced along his skin, his muscles, his chest, awakening and hardening every inch of his body. He kissed her lips, bit the side of her neck, nibbled her ear. Her moan, an approval of what he did to her, only made him crazy for more of her. He pushed down on the soap dispenser and lathered, from her shoulders, to her chest, he cupped her ample breasts. The sight of her wet, soft, and slippery curves in his hands was so addictive he could pleasure her like that forever. Her nipples puckered. She pressed herself into his palms. Her eyes closed in pleasure. He reveled in the knowledge of the intensity of her want. He wanted her just as much, or maybe even more.

Her hands slipped between his thighs. And what she did there right away became too much for him to maintain control. He held her wrists, stopping her before she'd take him all. He wanted to prolong his want until he'd made her come at least a few times first.

"Bedroom." His low growl surprised even him.

Showered. Dried. He pulled her over his shoulder, and she screeched and giggled, as he ran down the stairs toward their bedroom. *Their*.

Could there ever be a better vision than Eva lying

naked on his bed, waiting for him to claim her? Her hair splayed on the sheet, her lips waiting for his kiss, her breasts for his hands, her soft skin warmed for his hardened body...

He set his hands on her knees, spread her thighs wide, and dipped down to taste the gush of her wet warmth. He licked and tugged and sucked and pushed two of his fingers in and out of her. Her feminine fragrance enticed him to drive her to the edge. He grinned at how she arched her body, as though his teasing had become provoking but also delightful. Roused by her response, he held her clit between his thumb and index finger and wreaked havoc with his mouth until she screamed and called out his name. Her ecstasy, contagious, rolled through him like wind gushing through trees. It thrilled him to make her come undone for him. Her body, shimmering from sexual warmth, her expression blissful, her eyes provoking him for more, he *had to* see her like that, a few more times at least, before he, too, could let loose.

Chapter 7

Not wanting to be caged in his mother's home for a second more than he had to, he kept his routine simple. He stayed out all day. He walked the city. He slept on a bench in a park. Nearing dusk, he walked to the end of a pier from where he viewed the marina, his boat. How had his employer planned to signal him?

He returned to his mother's home only when exhaustion crept in, only when he'd been physically unable to wander any more.

Like he did every night before, he peeked out of each window that faced the street to check for anyone who might be watching him. Other than a couple of parked cars, with no passengers inside, and a few that drove past, the street seemed as usual. Boring. Nothing different.

With each evening he spent in his mother's house, his paranoia amplified.

He cut his gaze to the closet. *Someone there?* He picked up a large kitchen knife. Like the knife his mother had used to kill his father. He held it like she'd held. He approached the closet. Slow. Cautious. His heart nearly stopped to beat when he opened the door to the miniature room. Empty. He opened doors to all the closets in the house and left them ajar.

Bathroom. He approached the bathroom. Slow. Cautious. He kicked the door open so hard, the paint chipped at where his shoe had made impact. Empty.

He closed all the curtains to the windows. He shut off all the lights. Other than the flashing light from the TV, he let the rest of the house, and his mind, submerge in darkness.

He crouched into one corner of the living room. He hungered for revenge. Had it not been for his evil employer, he'd be in his boat. Cozy. Relaxed. His true home.

With gloved hands, he tugged a coarse-fibered rope tight.

He'd strangle his employer with it. He imagined the excruciating pain he'd inflict. He imagined his employer begging him for forgiveness. He imagined the immense pleasure those final moments of his employer's life would bring him.

*But...maybe...*he loosened the hold on the rope. Maybe he shouldn't kill his employer after all. What if Eva were to not leave her company? That may just be worse punishment than strangulation to his employer.

If not for the money, he wouldn't hurt Eva the way he did. Eva was a strong woman. Like his mother. Not as devious, though. Eva was special. He liked Eva.

The more he thought about her, the more he wanted to clean up his past mistakes. Maybe he should take up Eva's suggestion and reveal his employer's identity to her in exchange for immunity from prosecution? Maybe, he could take the money from his employer and also from Eva? Eva had offered to double what his employer would pay. His employer…Who was his employer? How did he not know the identity yet? He had to find out.

Yet another day he loitered the city. He slept in the park. He walked onto the pier. He gazed at his boat. But just as he did, he grew distracted by a woman who stood close to him. She tapped her fingers on the metal railing, and his attention fell to the rings she wore. Gold? Nah…*goldish*. From the corner of his eyes he could tell she'd been looking at him. Why? He didn't know. But, embarrassed that she'd caught him observing her rings, he looked straight ahead of him.

She opened her mouth to speak.

Why? What did she want from him?

"Hey." She smiled.

He didn't care to reply because…Was she a cop? Undercover?

What did she point to? His eyes followed her indicating to his arm. His tattoo. What about his tattoo? He studied her face. Nah…*not a cop*. He did not know how he came to that conclusion, but he was positive she couldn't be one of the undercover officers his employer warned him about. Regardless, he wouldn't take a chance.

***

Surreal to be sitting in an incognito FBI van so many years after leaving government work. Never once after Clive had taken over the Stanford business did he imagine the circumstance of this day. With a clear visual of the informant standing at the end of the pier, Clive and Trevor listened in on the conversation between him and an undercover female agent.

"Nice tattoo," she said to the informant, her voice, her expression flirtatious.

The informant held her gaze as he pulled down his sleeve.

The same eyes had watched Eva. The same hands had held that fake gun on her.

Clive tried his best not to rush out of the van and knock the guy's teeth out. A tough man-to-man confrontation would resolve it once and for all. But beating him to pulp, though it may quench Clive's fury, wouldn't let them charge the guy with offense for killing Eva's father, or for ruining her days since she'd taken over the company. Unless they caught him in the act of harming Eva, he'd remain free to hurt her at his leisure. That last part pissed Clive off so much, in a way it gave him the patience to hold back till they'd gather enough evidence to lock the informant up for life. So, instead, Clive quelled his urge to storm out of the van and shuffled a baseball from one hand to the other while the agent cast her trap.

"C'mon. Let me see it." She gave him a pretty grin, her lips deliberately painted in hooker red, as she called it.

The informant stared at her for a long second, long enough for Trevor to utter, "He doesn't trust her. He knows we're on to him."

"Good." Clive muttered.

"I guess. From what we know so far, he likes games. He'll play along."

"It's sexy." The agent persuaded.

A light smile broke on to the informant's features.

Something in the informant's look made him seem misunderstood, innocent somehow. It niggled at Clive that they hadn't zeroed in on whether someone else might be scheming, while the informant may only be a pawn.

The informant pulled his sleeve back up.

"A mermaid wrapped around an anchor. Is it supposed to mean something?"

The informant continued to stare at the agent in silence.

"Oh, I know. You own a boat. Is that why you have an anchor?"

Neither Clive, or Eva, or Trevor believed in

astrology, let alone tarot card reading. Yet, the incident with Mystique, when she'd barged into Eva's home one night, left them to leave no lead overlooked. Mystique had detailed to Eva, and later to Trevor, about the informant's visit to her parlor. She'd insisted she'd had visions of Eva on a boat. Though Eva did not own a boat, and Clive doubted she ever would given her near-drowning accident, they'd decided to throw in the question to the informant.

But…the informant didn't reply.

"Did it hurt?" She ran a finger over the tattoo.

He tugged his sleeve down, shoved his hand into his jacket pocket, and turned his head to look away from her.

"You know," she poked a red nailed finger at his arm, "I think I know you. I've seen you before."

He spun his head back to face her.

"You used to see a friend of mine."

"Who?"

"Candy."

The informant remained still, as though unaffected by mention of the woman he'd murdered.

"See." She turned the screen of her phone toward him. They had edited a photograph of Candy they'd found in her apartment. They added the female agent into the picture, her arm around Candy, both of them laughing, as though they'd been the best of friends.

Still no reaction from the informant.

"We worked in the same club."

"I don' go to clubs."

"No?" She pouted. "But I'm certain I saw you with her."

Again, no reaction from the informant.

It was her turn to look away. She remained silent long enough for him to take interest.

"You look nice. Both of you. Together, like that." He pointed a thumb toward her handbag where she'd tossed her phone.

"Yeah, we had some good times. She was my only friend. She was murdered, you know?"

"I need to go." He zipped his jacket up to his neck.

"Why? I was hoping we could go get a drink. My treat."

He smiled but didn't reply.

"How about tomorrow? Same time, same place?" she asked following him as he began to stride away from her.

"Maybe." He hurried away from the agent.

***

Trevor played the recording and they listened in to find clues from the conversation the female agent had with the informant.

A tight crease had formed between Trevor's brows. "He didn't deny knowing Candy." He muttered with spite. Trevor still blamed himself for not reaching her home fast enough that night. He could have saved her life. He could have caught the guy before he strangled her. Candy was innocent. She shouldn't have to die. He owed it to her to find the guy who killed her. That's the least he could do.

"Truth." The undercover agent clicked a button on the computer screen and entered their response. "He denied going to that club though."

"Lie." Trevor snarled.

"He didn't deny inking the tattoo hurt." The agent continued. "Truth."

"He didn't deny owning a boat." Clive added. Something about this whole boat thing irked Clive. He would never believe Mystique's prediction, but imagining Eva stranded on a boat, however impossible it may be, still bothered him.

"But we already checked. He doesn't own one. At least, there isn't one registered in his name or to anyone in his family, for that matter." The agent confirmed.

They stared at each other in silence for a long moment. As though that little exercise somehow gave Trevor the ability to read their minds, he gave the agent a nod, and she nodded back. He then gave Clive a nod. Clive nodded back…though he couldn't be sure what his friend might be up to.

Trevor pulled his cell phone from his pants pocket, tapped its screen a time or two, and held his phone to his ear. "Get me a list of names of boats and boat owners in the bay area. Especially look for any that may have an anchor, a mermaid, or anything similar in the names. Maybe it's painted on the boat. Maybe the upholstery. Dangling ornaments. Anything, anywhere, on a boat. Get this to me ASAP."

Chapter 8

She's in water…under water…like that time in the lake by her grandpa's house. But this time, it's not a lake, it's a pool. Clive's swimming pool.

"It's only four feet," Clive is saying to her. Which would be assuring, if she wasn't standing, but she is, and she's still under.

She tips on her toes. She raises her hands above her and stretches as far as she can. Still under.

She bends her knees and pushes the tiled floor below with the balls of her feet. She is traveling upward now. She is rising fast, but…still under.

Her breath is hastening. Wait, how is she breathing? And now that she's questioned it, her throat is closing, her chest is tightening, the water she is tasting is chalky, earthy…as if she were in the lake.

This cannot be happening again. How can this

be happening again?

The water is blue.

She blinks.

The water is gray.

Gray?

She blinked again.

The ceiling. Clive's bedroom. Clive's bed. Clive slept next to her. She exhaled her pent-up anxiety, relieved she'd once again awoken from her nightmare. She exhaled her fear. She exhaled her unease.

It had been slightly over one week since the informant's threat…one week since her uncle had given his notice…one week, two hours, fifteen minutes and forty seconds since that first moment she'd discovered Clive's swimming pool.

Every morning since, her eyes shot open at exactly three thirty. Sometimes being acutely aware of the pool after waking up, but most times being acutely aware of the pool in her nightmare.

Her routine, an unavoidable reoccurring annoyance, she'd become an expert at sneaking out of the bedroom in the wee hours of the morning, leaving Clive uninterrupted from his sleep.

With fatigued steps, she tottered to the kitchen and poured a glass of water. She tilted her head backward to drink, when her gaze met the ceiling. Strange how she'd been to the pool only once but had a precise awareness of how far and wide the pool spanned above her. Her gaze traced the layout. It covered the entire living room, part of the study and most of the kitchen. She stood under water. She stood under the deepest end.

She took a slight step back and leaned against a cabinet, slid down the veneer, and crouched on the floor. The water glass still clutched in her hands, her gaze still stayed glued to the ceiling.

I'm under water. I'm breathing. She took a deep breath. *I'm in deeper than the deepest end. I'm breathing.* She exhaled a slow exhale. *I'm fine.* She took another deep breath. *I'm fine.*

A sudden grab at her shoulder and she nearly jumped. "Clive! Oh—" She set a flat palm on her heaving chest, as though otherwise her heart would jump right out.

"Eva…" He knelt next to her, cupped her jaw in his warm palm, and brushed his thumb against her cheek. She pressed her face into his touch, letting him sooth her fright with each stroke. "You had that nightmare again?" He studied her with intense, concerned eyes.

Her hand trembled as she set the water glass on the floor. What had gotten into her? She dragged in a deep breath. She really had to rein her fear.

He pulled her to his chest. "Two sleepless nights in a row is not good, Eva."

She hated it too. Mostly, because she'd caused Clive to have sleepless nights. And, also, because lack of sleep had created havoc at work. Before this, she'd never been late to meetings, she'd never drunk coffee, and she'd never put off a lunch date with her friends…make that multiple lunch dates. Though she hadn't revealed it to Clive, she dreaded returning to his apartment after work each day. Not that the ceiling would break open and she'd drown. She had yet to let her anxiety brainwash her to believe that impossibility. Not that Clive would force her to swim. He'd be impassive if she never went back to the pool, *ever*. What did scare her then? She didn't know. But the awareness of being so close to water set in an irrational fear she couldn't justify even to herself.

"It wasn't as bad this time. I kicked the floor and pushed myself up in my dream, just like you suggested I should do."

"And you surfaced?"

She shook her head and regretted her answer right away when the worry in his eyes converted to a desperate need to banish her nightmare for good. "Maybe I will surface tonight when I dream again?"

Her words didn't bring any comfort to his strained expression.

He pulled her closer and nuzzled his face in her hair. "No. There won't be another night of this. We're staying at your place tonight. You've got to get some sleep. Also, I've found a really good therapist—"

What? No! No. No. No. "No." She nearly shouted against his chest. She pushed him away. "No."

A nerve twitched in his jaw. "Why not? You need to get over this." He, too, raised his voice.

"Yes. I do." She tried to sound as calm as she

could, because yes, she needed to get over this. "But I will in my own way."

"How?"

"By staying here, every night, and fighting it, one nightmare at a time."

He shoved his fingers through his hair and groaned. "C'mon, Eva." He rose to his feet, towering over her. "You need help. And I'll get you the best there is."

"No, you won't." She, too, stood. He still towered over her but seemed less intimidating than before.

She wanted to fight, she wanted to scream, she wanted to storm away from him, because he knew she did get professional help before, and it didn't work. If anything, it only made her think about her fear all the time. And she'd never return to that again. "Please," she stated, not questioned, *stated*.

He brought his hands to his hips, tilted his head down, and sighed. "I only want to help. I love you, dammit. I cannot let you suffer like this."

She placed a light kiss on his cheek. "I'm not suffering. Actually, I like the challenge. I fear less tonight than I did all last week."

That nerve in his jaw twitched again.

"I have to learn to handle this in my own way, Clive. And I'm near. I know it."

He looked away and shook his head. Of course he didn't agree with her. But he loved her, he respected her, and she'd always have it her way. "End of this week." His penetrating gaze met hers.

"I cannot let you suffer even one more night, but…" Worry strained his features. "End of this week. Please?"

"Okay." She half shrugged and kissed his cheek once more, oddly delighted that her challenge just got a bit more challenging. She needed any distraction she could to get away from the informant's fast-nearing deadline, away from the dilemma of who would take over after her, away from her uncle's retirement, away from her mother and Diane's incessant harassment about their wedding planning.

"Sunday it is."

"Friday it is." He no longer pleaded. He commanded. His tone, his expression, conveyed there would be no negotiating.

"Okay." She gave him a mischievous smile and headed toward the bedroom. Never would it have occurred to her that overcoming her fear of water in only two days would become a goal she'd enjoy accomplishing.

***

Next evening, leaving Clive in his study to take a conference call, Eva treaded up the stairs to the terrace garden. She'd worn the white one-piece swimsuit again. She associated her choice with being businesslike, her source of determination, concentration, and willpower that a relaxed two-piece suit, fit for a tropical vacation, wouldn't impart.

It took her over twenty minutes to step into the shallow end of the pool. That's how stupid her fear was.

It seemed easier when Clive had been by her side. She'd cling to him for her life, and he wouldn't have minded one bit, but she had to let go, she had to cling to herself, she had to free her fear *by herself*. Which in theory, made her courageous, like those women in warrior movies, the horse, the sword and all, facing a deathly blue, water dragon she had to slay. In reality, however, she crouched to her knees, letting the water spill slightly over her shoulders and froze when her mind took control and created a realistic illusion of the water rising up into a tidal wave, rising over her, past her...

Her heart pounded as though trying to run away from her, and maybe that's what caused those ripples, her hammering heart?

A warm hand squeezed her shoulder. She shrieked. Which again, in theory, should have comforted her, because who else would it be if not Clive? Instead, she flinched with such force, her hands fisted as though clutching on to the last shred of her life, she fell into the water and it splashed in turbulent waves all around her.

Clive laughed so hard she suspected he also cried a little.

She kicked his shin. Not too hard, though he feigned an "Ouch" as though it did hurt.

Right. She scowled her best scowl. "You've got

to stop doing that."

"But it's so much fun."

She swung her leg at him again, and this time with that dragon-slayer-warrior strength. Of course, she missed because he leaped into the water and free-styled away.

***

She tried out the pool one more evening, and then another. Each night she'd slept a bit longer than the previous, but each night she also dreamed that horrific nightmare that reset her anxiety back to the time she'd almost drowned. That Friday, after work, Clive drove them to her house, no questions asked.

That's how stupid her fear was.

Chapter 9

One more evening, he stood at the end of the pier. When his gaze fell on his boat...*that light*...in the navigation room...his employers signal? Had that light been on all these days and he noticed it only now? No. Couldn't be. It's the signal. Had to be. Yes? *Yes.*

Heat rushed to his face. He imagined a duffle bag overflowing with money. His heart leaped. He started to stride toward the marina.

His hurried steps turned to a jog and then a full paced run.

He'd never return to his mother's house. Never. Ever. That thought brought him a delight like no other. Not even knowing he was about to get paid made him that happy. But his euphoria lasted only for a second, because the next thought that raced through his mind came to him in his employer's

voice. *Why did you stay at your mother's, you idiot?*
He came to an abrupt halt. For an instant there, he'd
forgotten all about being followed. *That woman*, the
one who worked in the club. Had she followed him?
He turned around to check, but instead of the
woman, he found a large man charging toward him.
He'd noticed the man earlier taking photographs by
the pier. Had he taken photographs of him? Had he
seen him watching his boat these past days? Today?

He'd endured much for the sake of that *damn*
money. He was seconds away from getting paid. But
he couldn't risk getting apprehended now.

He took a stride back, and then one more that
adjusted his stance. He balled his fists tight. His
already hastened breath grew quicker.

He lifted his fists to his face. And when the man
neared to about an arm's length away, he swung at
him as hard as he could, only to miss him by inches.
He stumbled and fell sideways to the concrete.

The man, still running, had ducked in the nick of
the moment. "What the fuck, asshole?" The man
shouted as he ran past him toward an approaching
light-rail.

His chest heaved, his every muscle coiled, he
shook, unable to look away from the man or the
middle finger he raised as he stepped into the trolley
and rode past him.

Several judgmental eyes glared and glowered at
him. His heart sank into a deep void. He couldn't go
to his boat now that he'd attracted this much
attention. One or more of these people could be the
real ones following his every move. After his latest
gaffe, he couldn't tell who it may be.

Resigned and frustrated, he stomped away from the scene, away from his boat, away from his money, in the direction he never wished to take...toward his mother's house. Fuck. Fuck!

Chapter 10

As her uncle's last day at S. F. Designs fast approached, Eva decided, together they should make one last deal happen. It would be a memory for both of them to cherish. Besides, whether she'd continue to lead her company, or not, she needed this distraction.

Eva and her uncle worked overtime for several days, meeting with their design team, their suppliers, and their contractors, to cater to a new client from Europe Clive had introduced them to. Their hard work paid off when the client agreed to sign a ten-year deal with her company. "This was fun, any chance you could hire me back?" Her uncle had said.

***

Eva watched the glittering city convert to a blurry mess as her eyes filled with heavy emotion.

Amazing how with such short notice Tina had made all the necessary arrangements for her uncle's farewell. Everybody seemed to have a joyful time, excluding Eva. She'd thought no one noticed her escaping from the party to the auditorium patio. No one, except Clive, that is.

Her back was turned to him. Good. Otherwise he'd see the tears rolling off her eyes, which would mean he would want to know details, but she didn't want to even think about any of it right now, let alone speak. And that would only worry him more.

As luck would have it, before she could wipe the wetness off her cheeks, Clive circled his strong hands from behind her, around her waist, and pulled her close into his chest. He nuzzled her neck and rested his chin over her shoulder.

She sniffed, and the way he cocooned her even closer in that instant confirmed he saw right through her cover-up. He saw her sadness, even if she hadn't looked at him yet.

She turned her head sideways and placed a light kiss on the side of his face. His stubble prickled her lips in a way that would forever be sensual.

He brought his large hand to cup her jaw, and with the ball of his thumb he wiped some of the wetness from her cheek. His expression pained, she guessed what he was about to ask.

She kissed him once more. "I need some time for myself to regroup my thoughts. Please?" She sniffed again.

Her guess was spot on, because he didn't look happy, but he nodded.

"We'll talk. I promise. Just, not right now."

He nodded again but also straightened and turned her around to face him. "Who said anything about talking?" He dipped his head and went straight to kissing her.

She was confused that he did. She liked that he did. She loved that he did. Because only when his unique scent mingled with hers as his breath warmed the tip of her nose and then her mouth, and then when his soft lips met hers, did she realize how much she wanted to be distracted from what had been going on behind those doors.

Everyone who'd ever worked with her uncle, with her father, had attended the event. They drank. They laughed. They reminisced about the good old days, which were countless. A joyous but also melancholic occasion for many, especially for Eva, because starting this evening on, even if he may be only a phone call away, she still wouldn't have by her side the most dependable person she'd ever known or worked with.

So, yes, she wanted distance from all of it. And as he always did, Clive took away her every pain. She kissed him slow, she kissed him deep, and a light growl escaped him.

"Eva…" His hoarse tone conveyed his desperation. "I hate to take you away from here. But either that or we're doing it on this patio," he said, not bothering to hide his impatience.

That got her to laugh.

Minutes later, they were making out in Clive's car. She didn't know where they were headed other than "Half Moon Bay," the words Clive had said to Tom before raising the partition between them and the driver's section.

"Can he hear us?" She may have asked that before.

"No."

She doubted still.

"Soundproof," Clive asserted and pulled her into his lap.

The dim light that filtered in from the tinted windows amplified the sensuality of his hypnotizing eyes that clutched her soul, his hypnotizing hands that gripped and caressed her everything and everywhere, his hypnotizing words that provoked her with a litany of sexual promises, his hypnotizing mouth that brimmed nothing short of a raging desire in her to be claimed by him completely, fully. Nothing else mattered but that moment; nothing else mattered but her only wish to be spellbound by the sexiest man alive...*her* Clive.

Sometime that night, they'd arrived at a large house atop a cliff that dropped steeply to a narrow beach and strong crashing waves.

That Clive had planned to get her there for the weekend after her uncle's farewell touched her deep. How he'd foreseen she'd need to get away, she didn't know. Then again, Clive didn't really need a reason to pamper her to no end.

"Want to see me surf?" he asked that morning over a breakfast of warm croissants and fresh fruit.

"Yes." she answered per her first instinct. Second, though, reminded her about her irrational fear. "I—I..." She cleared her throat.

He laughed. "You can watch from a hilltop. There'll be a ton of rocks below, extending all the way to the water, which I promise, will be far, far away."

"You know I love the seaside." She could never forget the last time they drove down the coast. They had stayed on the beach for hours, watching kites and surfers. "I love the beach, like I love this house you picked for us to stay. The view is stunning. But, I cannot get into the water, that's all."

"The water doesn't even make it halfway over the rocks during extreme high tide."

"And today is extreme high tide?"

"Nope. Only high tide."

Well then, had she ever wanted anything more? "I can't wait to see you surf. Really." She nodded as she grinned.

He shoved his fingers into her hair, pulled her close and gave her a tight kiss.

An hour later Eva helped her sexy businessman fiancé morph into a sexy surfer boy. She drew the zipper of his wetsuit closed and kissed his cheek. "Be careful, okay?"

"I promise." He kissed her lips, once, twice, and then turned around to join his surf buddies he hadn't met in a while.

They paddled out into the ocean, over the mounting waves, away from the rocky shore, while she lounged on a beach chair, on the cliff, facing in the direction Clive went.

The bright light from the sun faked warmth at this time of the year. Eva pulled the hood of the red fleece jacket Clive had brought along for her over her head. She spread ten gloved fingers and both her palms around the cup of hot chocolate, letting every bit of warmth radiate through the porcelain, through the fabric, to her skin.

Her breathing raced, her body heated, her mind filled with joy, the first time, and every time after, that Clive took a wave. Her breathing stopped, her body cooled, her mind filled with fear, the first time, and every time, that Clive disappeared into the sea. If she reacted that way, how intense of an adrenaline rush must Clive sense as he surfed along the water? And each time he got back onto his surfboard, he waved at her and blew her a kiss. Like everything he did, he made this sport, too, seem effortless and fun.

Chapter 11

For the first time since he stayed at his mother's home, he didn't leave the house all day. He debated what he should do next. How could he make money and still get away, unharmed?

He should sneak out of his mother's house, hiding from whoever may be following him. Maybe he should pick a moonless night to run to his boat? His employer must have left his payment there. And once he'd find the money, what then? He should continue to stay low for a few days. Months? Years? No. *No.* He sprang from the couch and paced across the small house. How long should he hide? And what if he got caught?

He shoved a trembling hand into his pants pocket and brought out a cigarette pack. He ripped open the plastic film, tore off the paper lid, opened the foil, and pulled out a cigarette. He stared at it for a long moment. He'd never smoked before. He did not know what urged him to buy one of these yesterday, but he did. He paced to the kitchen, tugged at a drawer under the counter and picked up a box of matches. He pushed open the tiny cardboard tray, and one by one the matchsticks fell to the floor. He hadn't noticed before that he'd held the box the bottom side up. *Shit.* He knelt on the tiled floor. His hands still shaking, he picked up the matches a few at a time and shoved them back into the container. Just as he'd been about to light the last match he'd picked up, his eyes narrowed to the tip of the cigarette that extended from his mouth. *What am I doing?* He spit it out and let it fall to the floor. He threw the match and paced back to the living room.

He didn't want to go to prison. He didn't want to live his mother's fate.

The only way to go to his boat, unafraid, unharmed, would be to take Eva's offer.

He hated how little he knew about his employer. And the last time they spoke, he'd been instructed never to call that number again.

He pulled out the cigarette packet again. He pulled out another cigarette from it. He paced to the kitchen but came to an abrupt halt, where are those matches? He scanned across the floor and found it hidden between a small gap between the fridge and a cabinet. Back on his knees, he slid open the cardboard box, right side up, brought out a match and dragged the head over the side of the box. Didn't light. He struck it again. The tip broke and fell to the floor. "Shit. Shit!" He screamed. He hurled the box toward the wall with such force it opened, and the matches once again fell to the floor. He pulled out the cigarette from his mouth, ripped it to shreds, and as he did his gaze stuck to the small inscription imprinted nearing the filter.

That's when it occurred to him. He could hand over the money his employer left him to Eva. Maybe her fiancé could trace the notes to his employer, like they did in those crime movies. Yes. "That could work." *Yes.* His heart warmed. *That will work.* His freedom in sight, he grinned, but also cringed from how much his jaw hurt from gritting his teeth through all the stress.

Chapter 12

"So, which one?" Allie wiggled the dress against her chest.

Izzy, as usual needing to top Allie, held a dress against her chest, mimicking Allie, but she also added a pose and a twirl to her presentation.

"Uh…" Eva looked at Allie, then Izzy, and back to Allie, and then to the carpet. Yes, carpet, because, she couldn't care less what she wore to her wedding, let alone care about her friends' outfits. One, she'd never put much thought into imagining her wedding. Two, flowers, table settings, bridesmaid dresses, none of those were on her radar, *ever*. Three, they've been trying on dresses since nine this morning, and it was past noon. And four, she was so in tune with her interior design firm, *nice carpet*.

"Eva?"

"Hmm?" She slipped off her block-heel mule

and swiped one foot over the rug. Could this be the softest rug in the world?

"It's alpaca."

"Really?" Eva tilted her head and looked at the young saleswoman, who also happened to be one of the dress designers in the boutique Eva's soon to be sister-in-law, Claire, had suggested they visit. "It feels like I'm stepping on a giant cloud."

Izzy huffed. "See? This is what she does whenever we talk about her wedding. No fun at all," she grumbled to Allie.

"I know right? I think it's time for an intervention."

"I think so too." Izzy nodded. "Yeah. Should we ask the rest of her family to join?"

"I can hear you," Eva stared at her friends.

"Oh, can you? Which one then?" Allie flipped her wrist between her dress and the one Izzy held.

"I like them both."

Her friends fell silent. Good. It's settled then. Given it had been what…she glanced at her wristwatch… three hours fifteen minutes since they walked into this boutique. She sighed to herself. Who'd have thought their everlasting shopping session would come to an end after all?

"Eva, what's wrong?" Allie cajoled. "Don't you want to get married?"

Eva tilted her head back and groaned at the ceiling. Layers of ornate design circled a crystal chandelier. *Nice ceiling*. She sprang from her chair.

"I'm not discussing this again." She slipped off her second shoe, and with bare feet, she meandered along the length of the rug. When she reached the edge, she turned around and strolled back to her chair. "Wow, it's really like walking on feathers."

Izzy and Allie exchanged glances, communicating between themselves with their eyes. Given that Eva had participated many times in such wordless conversations with her friends, it wasn't much of a secret when together they hung the dresses back on the clothing rack, together they slipped off their shoes, together they strolled to the edge of the carpet and then back.

"We agree."…

"Like walking on feathers." Izzy picked the dresses from the rack, brought the one she liked to her chest, handed Allie hers, and asked, "Now, which one."

Allie wiggled. Izzy posed, twirled.

"Both."

"Oh, my God." Guess it was Allie's turn to groan at the ceiling. "Seriously?"

"Yes, seriously, and why not?" Because really, why the heck not? "I'm not into all that matchy-matchy stuff, and I would love for you to wear whatever you like."

"Really?"

"Yes. Really." Eva plopped back into the tufted velvet chair, brought the champagne flute to her mouth, and drank a long, effervescent gulp. Something about the tang from the fruity liquid mixed with the sparkling bubbles tingled her lips, her mouth, her throat. She could drink this all day. And today may just be that day, given the way her past few hours went. How were her friends not tired from slipping in and out of dresses all this time?

But back to the carpet, it would work well in their home library. *Their*. She smiled to herself. And this chair too. She rubbed the velvet. Maybe in a loveseat size? Also that chandelier. She tilted her head back to have another look at that ceiling.

"You know what would be ideal?" Izzy sounded dreamy.

"A refill?" Eva teased. They'd downed two bottles already, most of which Izzy and Allie drank.

Allie snorted a laugh.

Izzy poked her tongue into her cheek, but then nodded at the nearly empty glass in her hand. "Actually, yes, that would be wonderful. Could you, please?" She shook the flute at the saleswomen.

Izzy grinned at Eva as the woman topped her glass. "Thank you." She gulped down a sip, set the glass on the side table. "No." she said to Eva.

Oh, what now? A light grunt escaped her lips, and she met Izzy's stare.

"What would be ideal is if you were more into this. Because it is *your wedding*. But you aren't."

"Yes, exactly. And neither is Clive. *Therefore*, we asked our mothers to handle it." Why couldn't her friends get it? "We're more than ready for a simple marriage registration and a fun reception after."

"Then why are you doing this?" Izzy folded the dress in half and sat at the edge of a chair opposite Eva. Her one brow crinkled.

"For our families."

"Oh." Allie pouted a little, and she, too, sat at the edge of her chair.

Eva hated that without intending it, she'd somehow managed to bring down her friends' spirits. Whether she or Clive were into it or not, they both loved how much their friends and families were excited for them and were eager for their wedding day. "But, seeing you pick out these dresses makes me super happy. And again, I'll go with whatever you two want to wear. So, go ahead, surprise me." She hoped her friends believed her. Their enthusiasm did bring her genuine delight. She grinned, wide. They exchanged glances, and though slowly, she thought they might have been catching on. Guess not. She tried some more. "You know those dresses you tried earlier, think yours was royal blue," she said to Allie, "and yours"—she turned to Izzy—"was it a lemon yellow? I really loved those on you."

"Which one? Because I tried a yellow," Allie said.

"And I tried the blue," Izzy added.

"These." Eva rose from the chair, sashayed to the dress rack where hung the billion dresses her friends had tried, and pulled out the two dresses she spoke of.

"Oh those," they said in unison.

They hopped to their feet. "But how about these?" They held up the dresses they'd last tried and went back to examining their reflections in the mirror.

"These, too, look terrific."

They examined their reflections some more while Eva slid the dresses back on the rack. She strolled to her chair, plopped into it, and sighed to herself. She finished the last of her drink and set the empty glass on the side table. Before she knew it, the saleswoman refilled it. "Thank you."

And on the subject of enthusiasm, Claire rolled a squeaking clothing rack toward them, from which hung several white dresses. She pulled out two dresses and held up the hangers one after another to her chest. "So, which one?"

Dammit. If this were the first time Claire brought in dresses for Eva to choose, Eva would have been interested, excited, and whatever other emotion she imagined her friends and Claire would have liked her to be. But this was round three. Yes, two times before this Claire had rolled in the squeaky rack full of wedding dresses and by now, Eva couldn't distinguish one from another.

To her rescue, her phone buzzed. Before she'd even looked at the display, she knew exactly who was ringing her. After all, she'd instructed Trevor to call her at exactly twelve-thirty. She shot a quick look at her friends, making sure they were listening. Had they ever not snooped? She said enough to make it sound like something urgent was forcing her to leave and ended the call.

She slid the phone back into her purse, and when her gaze met with her friends again, she could swear they looked like she was about to tell them the wedding was off. "What?"

"We haven't tried all the dresses yet," Allie complained.

Of course, they hadn't. They'd only been there for three and a half freaking hours. Eva rose from her chair, keeping her action slow, her expression troubled, ensuring to appear as though she, too, hated to leave. In reality, she'd forgotten she had asked Trevor to rescue her, and receiving his phone call was the best she'd ever felt all morning. "I know, but it's past noon, and mom is waiting on those baguettes for lunch. And the seafood for the paella."

Allie pouted.

Izzy, seated on the chair, rested her elbow on her knee, and drummed her fingertips on her face.

She took their silence to indicate they believed her. Sweet.

Except Claire. She gave her a small smile and turned away to hang the dresses back on the rack, straightening the fabric as she went.

So she'd guessed what Eva was up to, but acted as though they had a tacit understanding to keep it a secret from rest of the party. Maybe Claire could help get them out of here faster than Eva could on her own.

"Or, we could stay back if you like. I can ask them to carry on without us." Eva added.

Before Izzy or Allie could respond, Claire

caught Eva's hint. "No. We should go. I'm famished." She winked only for Eva to see.

How could she not love her would be sister-in-law?

And how could she not hate herself for tricking her friends. Seriously, though, three hours and they hadn't decided on a dress they liked? Every dress in the boutique was too gorgeous to pass, Eva could close her eyes and pick one at random and it would be the best dress she'd ever worn.

"We're coming back later, though, right?" Allie asked.

"Of course."

"Cos I really like this one." Izzy held up the dress to inspect.

"Then get it," Eva couldn't believe they had returned to this conversation.

"But I like that one too, the blue one, that you liked. Actually, did you think the yellow would look better on me than on Allie?"

Argh!

***

They reached Eva's house at the same time Clive, Carter, Francis and Trevor arrived. Clive's disgruntled expression conveyed his tux try out went exactly like Eva's wedding dress selection. He rushed to her with long urgent steps. She rose on her tiptoes for a light peck, but he grabbed her arms, pulled her to his chest and kissed a long tight kiss.

Speaking of communicating with their eyes…

Let's get the hell out of here.

Let's.

Just as they were about to bypass the rest of the gang and head straight to Clive's car, Uncle Dave and Aunty Jamie got out of their car and started to walk toward Clive and her.

Eva's nose tickled at the whiff of booze that emitted from her aunt when she kissed her cheek. "I brought your favorite cake."

Aunty Jamie had to be the worst cook in the world. But the best baker Eva would ever know. Maybe because baking called for precision, in measurement, in timing, and could anyone be more detailed than her aunt? Always on time. Always the best dressed. Always the perfect smile. Obsessed with perfection, in mostly everything, except cooking, and her newfound addiction to alcohol.

Even the slightest intoxication morphed her aunt into an unfamiliar person. Aunty Jamie should have known that, and yet, she drank until she'd spilt her drink on her crisp ironed dress or her shiny toed pumps, or worse, on Uncle Dave. Which would bring him to utter the one sentence that for a fact gave her aunt nightmares, "No more for this one." He'd make light of the matter, and the others joined him. Her aunt, however, would give him a look filled with a mix of emotions. One of hurt from being betrayed by the love of her life, and also of regret upon realizing that despite all her efforts, like everyone else she, too, had flaws.

Eva never understood why her aunt hadn't resolved her addiction given how perfectly she portrayed her life to be otherwise. Regardless, she loved Aunty Jamie, for all the childhood memories and especially for all the cakes she baked for her.

The way Eva's day had gone so far, she was more than willing to skip all else and devour a huge slice of—her mouth watered at the thought—her aunt's famous chocolate debutante.

Clive cleared his throat as though to remind her of their escape from the wedding madness. And she couldn't fault him for that misjudgment. After all, he'd never tasted one of her aunt's cakes. "Aunty Jamie makes the best cake you'll ever eat." She swept her hand in the air as though that would somehow convince him of her affirmation. "*Ever.*"

"I bet she does." He gave her aunt a wide grin, and then tilted his head down and peered at Eva. "But, *we* have that *other thing* we needed to take care of, remember?"

He had no clue until he took that first bite. "This is two coats of bittersweet chocolate ganache poured over moist, dense chocolate cake we're talking about. We'll take care of that *thing*"—she nodded—"*after* we have that cake."

"Not the chocolate debutante, dear. I brought you the cheesecake."

"Oh, that too is out of this world good." She could have danced from the rush of joy that consumed her in that moment. She grinned at Clive.

He remained expressionless.

"Her cheesecake, New York style, but she tops it with a layer of homemade crème fraiche, you've got to…you absolutely *have to* try it." She gave him her best expectant look.

He raised his brows. *Are you sure you want to stay?*

She widened her grin. *Yes.*

He brought his arm around her waist and her shoulder bumped into his chest. He kissed her forehead. "Can't wait."

His sweet smile crumbled her heart. She did feel a little guilty for having changed their plan without giving him a chance for rebuttal. But he would for sure be delighted with her decision to stay back after tasting what may just be the world's greatest cheesecake.

Clive opened the door into the house from within the garage. Her aunt stepped in first, Eva waited for Clive to bring his arm back around her, and they followed after Aunty Jamie.

"I also made Jell-O cobb, my most recent creation." She grinned that perfect grin, her teeth pearly white against her signature red lipstick. "It's basically cobb salad, but, the best part, it's wrapped in Jell-O."

Eva glared at Clive and mouthed *don't eat that*. She reset her expression just in time for when her aunt looked over her shoulder and grinned again. "Maybe you could add it to one of your menu items in your restaurant. You're going to go back to being a chef, I assume?"

That question somehow always dropped a bowling ball in her gut. "Yes." And she left it at that, not elaborating. Whether or not she ever opened her dream restaurant, there would be no way she'd add her aunt's Jell-O cobb to any menu.

"Maybe your uncle can take over from you. I know his last day is near, but deep down in his heart, I think he wouldn't mind leading the company if you choose to concentrate on restaurant business. Just saying." She half shrugged.

Eva wouldn't doubt that. She always thought her uncle more deserved to lead S. F. Designs than her.

"You know, I don't know why it didn't occur to me to bring you the chocolate debutante too. Maybe I'll bring it over to your work one of these days? For an afternoon tea break? What do you think?"

"Oh, aunty, that's so sweet of you. But you really don't have to. I mean, you've already put so much effort for today—"

"Eva, dear." She stopped walking and faced Eva and Clive. "I'll pick a day when I have to be in the city anyway. It's really not a problem. Besides, you know how much I love baking." She smiled her signature caring smile, and wooed Eva right in. "And then who knows? Maybe you'll pick it to be your wedding cake?"

Her aunt really was the best. Eva kicked herself for having judged her salad before even giving it a try. "There's a strong possibility that your cake would be our top pick." She tilted her head to look at Clive. He grinned a sexy grin of approval.

***

Eva walked with her aunt into the kitchen, while a reluctant Clive got tugged away into the living room by his brother. They each craned their necks to keep their gazes connected for as long as they could, but the opaque walls became their undefeated enemies. When she lost sight of Clive, Eva sighed to herself and gave her mother a hello kiss.

"Did you pick out your dresses?" her mother asked.

"No, we didn't," Allie grumbled. "We had to bring these." She handed the large brown paper bag to Diane. Loaves of bread peeked from its opening.

"Oh, they smell so fresh."

"Uh-huh," Allie replied to Diane but narrowed her gaze at Trevor. "If you went with them"—she pointed with her thumb in the direction Clive and Carter had gone—"how did you know they"—she pointed at her mother and Diane—"were waiting on the baguettes and seafood? And why didn't you go buy them yourself?"

Uh-oh.

Trevor. The FBI agent. They must have trained him for this sort of interrogation. Eva stared at him. But the way he stared back... Deer. Headlights.

Eva cut a look to her mother. *Mother? A little help?*

"Diane, how do you like this wine?"

"It's delicious. And wait, did we drink it all?" Diane laughed as she tilted the bottle into her glass and the last few drops trickled out.

"Evie, get us a couple more bottles from the cellar, will you?"

"Will do." *Thank you, Mama.* She gave her mother's cheek another kiss and rushed out of the kitchen.

"Let me help." Trevor followed her out.

They strode past the living room, and just as they were about to turn toward the steps to the cellar, Clive hurried toward them. "Where you going? Take me with you."

***

Eva poured them each a full glass of wine. She tasted the maroon drink. "Mmm. This *is* good. Yeah?"

Clive and Trevor sipped their drinks.

"Mmm."

"Yeah."

Clive and Trevor nodded.

"I know you two are done talking wedding stuff, but…this is a really good choice for wedding dinner wine." Trevor said.

"Yeah." She nodded.

"Yeah." Clive agreed, but stared at the drink in

his glass.

Maybe he wanted to pick a Stanford wine instead? "Would Carter mind?" Eva asked.

Clive picked up the bottle from the wooden table and read the label. "I don't think so. If anything, he might just consider buying the vineyard." He added a cocky grin.

They'd stayed in the wine cellar for as long as they could, half an hour at best, but it seemed a little under two minutes, when Izzy yelled from somewhere in the house, "Lunch is served. C'mon to the patio."

They each grabbed a couple of bottles of wine and joined the family.

***

"Mmmm, this paella is delicious." Typical of Clive to be the first to appreciate. Typical of her mother to give Clive a smile filled with adoration. Eva loved that her mother loved him too.

"Yes, the best I've ever tasted." Trevor added. "Thanks for inviting me, Mrs. Avery."

"Please, call me Julie. And I'm overjoyed that you were able to join us."

"What's this green thing?"

"Oh, cilantro. Eva introduced me to it." Her mother's eyes filled with adoration for Eva this time. "She told me it goes on everything. And it really does."

"Interesting flavor. So, how long did it take you to make this?"

Their conversation went on for minutes as her mother gave Trevor every detail of how to cook the perfect paella, from what pan to use, to what ingredients to buy from where, to when and how to add in the seafood. And all that time, Trevor gave her mother his undivided attention as though he really would re-create the recipe just by memory.

"I see where you get your cooking streak." Clive nudged Eva's shoulder with his.

There was something more in his expression other than the obvious compliment.

"We need to leave." He kept his tone low and serious.

"We *so* do."

"Why can't you two see the fun in this?" Eva couldn't imagine how her mother had caught their whispering over the loud laughing and talking going on around them, but she had, and she sounded as though all her adoration for Clive and Eva had vanished in that instant. "It's a once in a lifetime thing. Well, hopefully."

Her mother's tone set off an alarm in Eva's mind. A tone she'd been accustomed to since her childhood. A tone that indicated her mother wanted her way, no questions asked. Eva had to reset her mother's mood before she got all weepy and out of control. "Of course, it is, Ma, both, fun and once in a lifetime." Eva set her fork and knife on opposite sides of her plate, lugged the napkin from her lap, and dabbed her mouth. "But too many options are sometimes too much. And you and Diane are doing so well with the planning." She leaned back into her chair, picked up her wineglass, brought it to her lips, and pulled in a long sip. Mmm, definitely wedding wine.

"Sure, we are. But there's only so much we can do. In the end, it's up to you both to decide from the options we've narrowed down for you."

"And we will." Eva rushed her agreement, but suspected her mother had already made up her mind not to listen.

"You want simple, pick simple. But don't elope or something, because I've waited for this for a long, *long time*." Her lips quivered and she set her silverware on her plate.

"Me too." Diane chimed. She, too, laid her silverware on her plate.

There would be nothing Eva could do about where this conversation would head next. It seemed as though her mother and Diane had planned this intervention.

Great. Just great.

Their conversation had silenced the table, and everyone's attention narrowed in on Clive and Eva.

"You too, what?" Francis asked Diane, and then bit into a scallop.

"Tell them not to elope, Francis." Though neither Clive nor Eva had ever considered eloping, Diane made it sound as though they had, and Francis would be the only person left on this planet who could stop them.

Francis very nearly coughed his food out.

"You're eloping?" Izzy and Allie chimed in unison.

"No wonder she didn't want to plan her wedding." Izzy went on.

"Or pick a dress." Allie added.

Someone gasped an unusually loud gasp.

Eva and Clive turned to glare at the source of the deliberate attempt to instigate drama. *Joey?* Because since when did her brother gasp?

"Eva, is that true?" Of course, Joey wouldn't miss a chance to cause more trouble. Of course, he'd match his tone with her friend's hysteria.

She shook her head at him. And, he grinned with a familiar mischief.

"Wait, who's eloping? What did I miss?" Carly, Claire's twin sister, older than her by mere minutes, walked into the patio from having tucked Emma in for her afternoon nap.

"Clive is." Trevor grinned. They shouldn't be surprised by Trevor's deception either, given that the sole purpose of his friendship with Clive revolved around adding fuel to any fire that would get his best buddy into trouble. His grin mimicked Joey's, and he bit into a slice of garlic bread.

"I hope you choke," Clive grumbled.

Unaffected by Clive's curse, Trevor said to Carter, who also shared the same level of delight in shining the wrong kind of spotlight on Clive, "Isn't this good?"

Carter, too, bit into a slice of bread. "Mmm, this *is* good."

"Thank you. At least you boys appreciate us stopping Clive from eloping," Diane said.

"Wait, with Eva?" Carly asked.

"Who else?" Izzy and Allie chimed.

Carly filled her plate with food and took a seat. "Well then, what's the problem?"

Diane gasped. "Carly Diane Stanford!" She threw her disheveled napkin on her plate. "How can you not want to see your brother get married?"

And that was the turn the rest of the family get-together lunch took.

After lengthy discussions that neither Clive nor Eva partook in, Clive, too, threw in his napkin. *Like his mother.* "We might as well elope." No one else heard but Eva, because everybody else's voices had risen to a decibel that allowed them to go about in their own delusional chaotic revisions and manipulations of when, why, and how Clive and Eva had planned to elope.

Clive took a huge gulp of his wine, and as he savored and swallowed he tilted his glass. He peered at the liquid inside.

A beautiful, rich. "Burgundy," she mumbled.

"What's that?"

"The color."

"Of what?" He gave her a blank look.

She grinned. Her otherwise razor-sharp

influential businessman was too cute when clueless about basic things, like colors. "What were you looking at?"

"Your hand."

"Oh." One moment she gazed at a pinkish hue that fell on her hand splayed flat on the table, and the next she cupped it with the other and pulled to her chest. Odd how after spending many months with Clive, even today the slightest attention from him, spiked her heartbeat and made her shy.

"No. Put it back there."

With reluctance, she returned her hand to the table and Clive dragged it in position, closer toward him.

"Look through the glass."

She leaned toward him and peeked as he indicated.

The stone on her engagement ring glowed a beautiful hue of pink from the afternoon sun that fell into the glass, through the wine, on her hand. "Oh wow." And she had no idea how or why, she muttered, "Wedding dress color?"

He gave her a look as though to say she'd read his mind. He pulled her hand to his lips, placed a sweet kiss and set it in his lap. "Wedding dress color." He nodded, smiling.

They returned to staring at their animated family and friends.

"Are we like them?" Eva asked, keeping her voice low for only Clive to hear.

Diane sniffed as she dabbed her eyes with a tissue Francis had pulled out of his pocket. He pulled another one out and handed it to Diane. She passed it to Eva's mother. And she, too, dabbed her eyes.

Uncle Dave stared at nothing in particular. While Aunty Jamie topped her glass for the hundredth time.

Joey stood behind their mother, rubbing her shoulders, as though that would calm her from crying. Otherwise, he laughed with Trevor and Carter at what must have been the funniest joke ever, because they laughed, and laughed some more.

The way Izzy and Allie leaned in toward each other, they had to be talking about those dresses again.

Claire brought in a neither awake nor asleep Emma, who'd circled one plump hand around her aunt's neck and suckled the thumb of her other.

Carly swept her fork along her plate in long quick strokes and gobbled down the last of her lunch.

"I think I was adopted," Clive said.

"I think I was too." Eva nodded.

Clive ate the last of his cheesecake. "Wedding cake?"

"Mmm, totally." She, too, emptied her plate.

Clive took another huge gulp of wine and almost emptied his glass. He tilted his glass once more and stared at the last of the liquid left within. "Wedding wine then?"

She took a huge gulp. "Wedding wine."

They clinked their glasses, their eyes trained on each other, then finished their drinks.

Something between them made it a moment only for them to share. A moment when everyone around her, except Clive, had vanished.

Eva didn't think, because she didn't want to. Eva didn't speak, because she didn't want to. Eva didn't breathe, because she didn't want to. Because here she was imagining her wedding dress, picking her wedding wine, her wedding cake, all of which in her mind didn't affect her life with Clive in any way, but that she had made those choices *with* Clive, had made that moment special. Fancy wedding or not, she'd love Clive forever.

She couldn't distinguish between the effect her thoughts had on her and the effect of Clive's peering at her in that certain way that told her he wanted her more in that moment than he'd ever wanted anything else. Did he really look at her that way? Or did her conspiratorial mind imagine it all? Whichever it may be, she wouldn't deny she needed him. "Let's…"

He leaned in and kissed her and left her with a light but suggestive bite. She swallowed hard.

He smirked a playful grin. "You have no idea how badly I want to."

Eva cocked her head to hide her delight behind her hair from whoever else at the table might be watching. Yes, a huge high-five yes, *let's get outta here*. She pushed her chair back and rose.

Clive, too, stood from his seat. He gave her his arm, and she held on to his bicep. They cut each other a gaze, and smiling, they left the party, unnoticed.

***

The elevator dinged, and the doors opened to the foyer that led to Clive's apartment. They'd already been making out on their drive to his apartment, during their wait for the elevator, on their way up in the elevator, her fingers gripped at his hair, his hands shoved up her dress, they kissed long and hard only to break away for a quick needed breath when the doors dinged open to the penthouse level.

He lifted her up and she wrapped her legs around his hips. He stepped out of the elevator car, pushed her to the nearest wall, and pressed into her. A light gasp escaped her lips and she surrendered to his urgency.

Craving for each other had become an obsession. They were so in tune with each other's desires, nothing went amiss between them. The pulse in her throat pushed to her skin, and he kissed her right there, unleashing a shiver. His fingertips lifted her dress that he had already pushed to the top of her thigh. Reading his mind, she gripped the satin edge with both hands and pulled it up and over her head in one quick swoop.

His face glowed with mischief when a quiet laugh escaped him. Not liking his mocking her earnestness, she gave him a stern look. He cleared his throat. Letting a smile linger on his face, he leaned in to kiss her. But she kept her lips sealed. He cajoled her with light kisses and bites, continuing until her longing overruled her protest. Deciding to take revenge soon, for the time being, she yielded to his will.

He slipped one finger under the side of her thin waistband. Tearing her underwear had become a tell-tale sign of his horniness.

"I'm gonna start wearing boy-shorts," she mumbled against his lips.

He pulled back to meet her eye. His brows furrowed, his expression questioned, he tugged at the waistband. "They have this?"

"Nope. They have this." She reached into the side of his trousers and yanked at the elastic of his briefs.

Now *he* gave her a stern look.

Ah...the sublime bliss of revenge...A light laugh escaped her this time.

He muttered something under his breath, and with one harsh tug he cut free the thin strap of her thong. The thrilling action had them kissing again, with more aggression than before.

His large, seeking hands roamed over her ears, her neck, her shoulders, her arms...the effect an outburst of devastating desire. And hers fussed with the buttons of his shirt, which in that moment seemed far too many. Just as she considered that ripping the fabric off would be easier, he pulled away from their kiss, undid the remainder of the buttons, peeled his shirt off his body, and threw it to the floor.

He pulled her hard against him, stepped in closer to the wall, and they returned to kissing. Satisfaction fluttered her insides from how fast he'd catered to her unspoken need. She roamed her fingers over his chiseled chest, strong shoulders, his smooth neck, his grip-worthy hair. Forgetting everything and everyone, she immersed herself in that moment with Clive.

Once breathless, they pulled back from kissing, leaned their foreheads against each other, and panted.

"I can never have enough of you." His whisper sent a delightful hunger to every erogenous part of her heated body. She could never have enough of him either.

"Me…you…"

His fingers dug into her hips, telling her how much her passion flooded voice, soft by his ear, had turned him on. She used the cue and mouthed his sensitive nerve endings until he once again muttered something, tugged at her hair and tilted her head to an angle he wanted, and went back to kissing with a desperation like never before.

His lips ravaged her mouth and then trailed down her chin, her neck, and clamped down exactly where she craved him the most. He tugged and rolled her strained nerves with his lips alone. Exhilaration flooded through her, and she lost all coherent thought. She wanted more of him. She wanted all of him. She arched her back, pushing farther into him. He squeezed her breasts together with his hands and pillaged one after another with his mouth. Her senses overwhelmed, she closed her eyes and submerged into the unbridled pleasure.

Just as she longed for it, he thrust up into her silken wet heat. Her legs tightened around his waist, her toes curled toward the balls of her feet, her breath hitched in place, as he filled her aching void. He stopped only for a second, and before he asked, she rushed her words, "I'm fine." He studied her for a second more.

She didn't understand what he wanted, but then he moved ever so slightly, as though to let her stretch to accommodate him. She smiled at his concern for her. "Thank you."

"Good?"

She nodded.

He grinned, convinced. He held a strong arm around her waist to stabilize. The other he cupped behind her head to shield her from the concrete wall and he withdrew only to thrust higher into her. She gasped as his hot width filled every inch of her. He went on with the rhythm, and her only responses were moans of pleasure each time he pushed. The position in which he took her should have been tiring, because the veins in his neck and his biceps strained, but his expression conveyed the opposite. His face etched in sexual lust, while his greenish-blue irises turned dark with desire. He kept his gaze locked with hers. Did she look at him like he did at her? A thrill sprang from within her gut at that realization. Their faces neared, and he kissed her, not his usual kiss. He kissed her slow. He kissed her special. He kissed her sensual and sexy, as though any harder and she'd break. He stilled. He pulled back.

She didn't understand the concern in his expression. "What?"

"Are you really marrying me?" The hoarseness in his tone conveyed more than his disbelief. He'd told her once that he never thought he'd find anyone after Olivia. And especially not Eva. Just like she never thought she'd find anyone after Jake. And yet here they were, Clive and her, in each other's arms, willing to spend the rest of their lives, and beyond, together.

"How can I not?" She kissed him this time, and he let her for a second or two before taking over.

He gathered her tighter into his arms and walked them from the foyer to the couch in his living room.

He laid on top of her and thrust himself back in. Her every nerve revitalized at their connection. All slowness gone, he reverted to taking her deep and hard. Each time he met that spot, she screamed in delight. He went on and on, until together, they lost focus and plummeted into an amazing oblivion. They breathed hard and heavy against each other's necks. Seconds later, he rolled off her and draped one hand under her neck, around her, and tugged her close. She rested her face against his chest, listening to his racing heartbeat as it slowed to normalcy against her ear.

He nuzzled his nose into her hair. "What's that? I love that."

"Gardenia."

"It's a...?"

"Flower."

He dug his face into her hair again and inhaled a deep breath. "Wedding flowers?"

She grinned against his chest. "Wedding flowers."

Chapter 13

"Eva."

Trevor's tone too serious for her to go with a hello, she instead asked, "What's up?"

"Where are you?"

"In my office. Why?"

"He's walking toward Stanford Tower."

The informant. Though they were damn near his one-month deadline, and he hadn't delivered the note yet, Clive had suspected he'd try to meet her at least one more time before that final date to ensure she would leave the company after all. Given how adamant Clive had been about the possibility of her never meeting the stalker ever again, no way he'd approve of her playing the bait. "You want me to head down?"

Trevor did not reply.

"Clive doesn't know about this, does he?" she

asked.

"I left him a voice mail."

"Yeah, he's out with a client."

He fell silent again.

"I'll leave now."

"Clive won't like this, Eva."

"I know. But he'll understand why we had to do it. And you'll be watching me, right?"

"Absolutely. I'll be right there. So will Mike, I've already alerted him. I also have a few of my guys. We will all be there."

She pulled in a deep breath. Her insides quaked as she did. Her words conveyed strength, but her mind brought back the memory from their ski trip. She almost relived the moment he'd pointed the gun at her. A shiver rushed through her. She pulled in another deep breath and stood from her office chair. "Okay. I'll head down, and what?" She started toward the door.

"Go to the coffee shop."

She pulled her office door open. Tina looked at her from behind her desk. Maybe she should take Tina along for support? A grim image of the informant pointing a real gun at them rolled through her mind. *No.* She couldn't take Tina. She had to go alone.

Tina stood from her seat, as though she assumed she should accompany her. It had been their usual afternoon tea break time. Eva shook her head and added a quick smile, which Tina didn't buy. Her brows shot together, and she mouthed to Eva, "Is everything okay?" How could she tell? Eva gazed at her reflection in a mirrored wall. She'd never looked this pale. She glanced back at Tina and gave her a wide grin. She had to act natural. With Tina, with everyone. Because the informant would be watching her, and they had to catch him this time.

Tina bought her act, grinned right back, and returned to her desk.

From inside the elevator Eva stared across the S. F. Designs lobby at Tina. Maybe this would be the last time she'd see her secretary, her friend. That morbid thought rushed a painful emotion from her chest. She exhaled. She gulped. The elevator doors closed, and she rode down the building, alone. She had nothing to fear. Trevor would be there. But she missed Clive. She brought out her cellphone and texted, *I love you.*

She stared at her phone for Clive's response until the doors dinged open. No reply.

She slid her phone into her pants pocket. With heavy steps, and a racing heart, she strolled across the vast lobby, and headed toward one of the entrances to the coffee shop from inside the building. She tried not to appear as though she was searching for familiar people, but she searched hard. Other than the building security, who waved at her, and she waved back, she found no one she recognized. Where's Trevor? His agents? She entered the coffee shop with a cautious step. Where's Mike? Where the heck is everybody? Did something go wrong? Was the plan still on? She should check her phone. She pushed one hand into her pants pocket. Or maybe not. What if the informant had been watching? She needed to play it cool.

She dragged in a deep breath and stood in line to place her order. She didn't want to drink. She didn't want to eat.

"Jasmine tea, please. And an almond biscotti." She smiled at the cashier. He smiled back. She didn't recognize this guy. New maybe? Or maybe one of Trevor's agents?

Seconds later he handed her a porcelain cup with piping hot water. Uncanny how the bubbles that rose from the inserted tea bag matched what her insides did at this moment. She exhaled. Maybe she should not go through with this. Maybe this had been a terrible idea. What was she thinking? This definitely was a terrible, terrible idea. *Oh, my God.* She licked her lips. *What am I doing?* She licked her lips again.

"Here's your biscotti." He laid it flat on the space between the saucer and the cup.

She should thank him, but she couldn't. She should pick up her drink, but she couldn't.

"There's a table for you right there, *Eva*." He said in the softest tone. He knew her name? One of Trevor's men. A rush of relief undid her knotted insides. She turned her head and glanced behind her to look for the table and found Mike. He set a briefcase on an empty table across from where he sat, bent down and started to tie his shoelace.

"Thank you!" Not for the drink or the cookie...but for revealing himself...*thank you, thank you, thank you.* Heat rushed to her face. Though she remained tense about encountering the informant, finding that Trevor had kept his promise to protect her gave her the right amount of confidence she needed to pick up her drink and head to the table.

Mike had finished tying his shoelace. He pulled his briefcase toward himself when Eva arrived at her table. Just when she placed her drink on the wooden counter, someone gripped her arm tight and she screeched.

Her insides hollowed. Her stomach churned. She could throw up. "Aunty Jamie!" She almost screamed and gathered a few suspicious looks from others seated around them.

"Oh, my God. I didn't mean to scare you, dear. Are you okay?"

"Yes." She shouted and cringed when she gathered more stares. *Shit.* She let out a quick hesitant laugh. "Ah…" She tried hard to catch her breath. "Yes. I'm okay." She nodded and laughed some more.

Her aunt gave her a blank stare.

"Cappuccino for Jamie." The barista called out her name for drink pickup.

"Let me get my drink, and I'll join you."

Before she could think of a way to avoid her aunt, Aunty Jamie paced toward the cashier. Eva cut a quick gaze to Mike, who was staring at his phone. Phone. Oh, right. She pulled her phone from her pocket and sat at her table.

Trevor: *Don't worry about Jamie.*

How could she not? She replied: *What if he hurts her?*

Trevor: *He won't.*

How could he be so sure?

Trevor: *We won't let it come to that.*

Trevor: *How are you doing?*

Eva: *Terrified. Otherwise I'm doing just fine.*

He sent her a smiley emoji.

Trevor: *She's heading your way.*

Eva took the hint and slipped her phone back into her pocket.

***

"How are you doing, dear?"

"Good. And you?"

Her aunt studied her face, as she dragged a chair and sat across from Eva. "You didn't look good a second ago."

"I was distracted. Sorry. I shouldn't have screamed."

"Oh, it's not your fault. I shouldn't have grabbed you that hard. Your uncle complains about my grip all the time. It's too strong for him. Can you believe that?" She laughed.

Eva found no humor in anything at the moment. But, she laughed back.

"What are you doing here?"

"Since it's your uncle's last week here, I thought I should pick him up. Not many people know this about your uncle: he's a very emotional guy. Glad, at least one of us is." She laughed again.

Again, Eva laughed back.

Just then something shifted in her aunt's expression. She couldn't pinpoint what. Like she saw someone she recognized.

"Don't look back, but I think there's a man here watching you."

Eva's stomach did a tumble. "Watching me?" Must be one of Trevor's men.

Something shifted further in her aunt's expression. Eva still couldn't pinpoint what.

"He looks nervous somehow. Like he…" Her aunt's expression blanked. "He wants to talk to you," she said tightly.

Informant.

Not moving her head, Eva cut her gaze to Mike. He gave her a brief glance, and then the slightest nod. The informant.

She exhaled. Maybe he wouldn't approach her as long as her aunt stayed with her. Maybe she should approach him instead? "I need a napkin. I'll be right back." Eva slid her chair and just as she had been about to get up, her aunt clutched her forearm so tight Eva would have screeched again, from pain, and not fright this time.

What had gotten into her aunt? Was she drunk

again?

"Don't go." Her aunt didn't ask, she ordered.

"What? Why?"

"I don't like the way he's looking at you."

"What way?" She had been about to turn her head to look, but her aunt tightened her bony fingers around Eva's arm. "You're hurting me."

She loosened her grip but continued holding on to Eva.

"Wait. He saw someone. He's leaving." Her aunt turned her head toward the door that opened into Stanford Tower. Eva, too, looked in that direction.

Clive.

***

The second Clive heard Trevor's message about the informant heading toward Stanford Tower, he'd cut short his offsite meeting and called Trevor while Tom raced him back to be with Eva.

"What the fuck? I thought we had a clear understanding that no matter what, Eva would never see this guy again," he screamed into his phone.

"I'm sorry, man. I don't like using Eva as bait just as much as you don't, but given the situation, you would have done the same."

The fact that he would have didn't change how frightened he felt right now for Eva's life. He clutched the phone hard, as though Eva's life depended on it. "Where is she?"

"Just entered the coffee shop."

"And the informant?"

"He, too, just walked in."

"Fuck!"

"A lot of people are watching her." Trevor assured.

"Except me." He grunted.

"Where are you?"

"Seconds away." A few very long seconds. Anything could happen in a few seconds.

"She wanted to do this, Clive."

"Of course, she did. That's who she is. And *that's* what I fear the most. I'm here." He cut the call, slid the phone into his pants pocket and charged toward the coffee shop.

Eva sat at a table, with her aunt, and Mike sat at a table adjacent to them. One glance and Clive had spotted all the undercover agents, the cashier, the girl mixing the drinks, Trevor...Clive did a double take when his gaze met his friend's. A fake mustache, thick glasses, hair—hair? He'd been born bald.

Funny how his friend looked.

Not funny how the informant stared at Eva.

Just as he pushed the coffee shop door open, the informant got up from his chair and paced out of the door facing the street.

Clive cut a look to Mike, a signal for him follow the guy. He rose, picked up his briefcase, and stalked after the informant.

And before Clive knew it, Eva sprung into his arms, her body as cold as his. He held her close, he held her strong, he held tighter than he'd ever held her before.

Chapter 14

Eva seemed less worried after the coffee shop incident. She trusted the security detail Clive had set for her. She trusted that neither he nor Trevor would let her have another one of those horrid encounters she'd had with the informant in the past. Her calm made Clive worry less. But he remained observant at all times. He watched out for whoever spoke to Eva, whoever walked past her, whoever glanced at her whether casual or lingering. He memorized them all, their faces, their gestures, everything he could decipher. Eva called it overkill, but he would do no less to protect the one person who mattered to him more than anyone he'd ever known.

The door to his office opened. His secretary peeked in. "Mr. Stanford."

He didn't know anyone who'd won a lottery, but the way Trish grinned, maybe she had won. After all, she'd bought two tickets every week for the past forty years. "What's up?"

"She's here." Trish beamed as though he should know whom she referred to.

Eva? No, why would Trish announce her? Because she'd walk right in. "Who?"

Her excitement turned to a dark frown. "Your ten o'clock." The door clicked as she pulled it closed behind her. She walked with caution toward his desk.

He still didn't know whom Trish referred to, but it had to be someone she liked. "O-of course." He nodded. "I've been waiting." No he hadn't. "Please, do bring *her* in."

Trish narrowed her eyes. "You have no idea who, do you?"

"Not a clue." He tried his best grin. That grin could make anyone swoon is what Eva would say about it. Didn't she know that sort of a compliment only strengthened his ego? Yes, he liked being overconfident. His grin moved boulders. And any moment now, Trish would giggle and let him in on whom she had been excited for him to meet.

Any moment now.

He continued to grin that grin, but somehow felt stupid about it. Had he lost his charm? Did it work on Eva at least?

Trish's glare warned him to straighten in his chair, because he recognized that look from the many times his mother looked at him that way. Like that one time when she'd asked, "What do you mean you forgot to pick up your sisters from school?" Yes, he'd done that once, maybe twice, during his teenage years. The first time he forgot on account of getting his first ever blowjob, and that, too, from one of the hottest cheerleaders in his school. Not the time to be thinking about his sisters. And the second time. *What had happened the second time?* Same cheerleader?

"Mystique," Trish stated, widening her eyes, if only slightly.

That name reeled his attention to the present. "Why am I meeting Mystique?"

Trish tried to stifle her gasp, but with all his attention jolted back to guarding Eva, Clive wouldn't miss the slightest of vibes. He hadn't meant to sound harsh, and he hated not to have shown more restraint, but Mystique had been on his radar since the time she'd visited Eva at her home. Although she had cooperated with the investigation—she'd recited, not once but many times, every and any detail they'd wanted to know about her encounter with the informant—neither Clive nor Trevor were convinced she wasn't involved somehow.

"I wouldn't know, Mr. Stanford." Trish took a few unsure steps closer to his desk. Her mind control power vanished, and she worried her lip between her teeth. "Sorry. I should have asked when she made the appointment. I assumed you wanted to meet her. Because—" She clasped the edge of the chair back with both her hands. Her knuckles turned whiter with every passing second. "I meet her every month. I trust her predictions a hundred percent. She has many followers. And I—I assumed you wanted to, you know?"

No, he didn't. Because how could anyone believe the future could be foretold? Because if it could, he would never have lost Eva only to meet her again fifteen years later, he would never have gone out with Olivia, and he would never have let her die the way he had. The informant would never have come into Eva's father's life. Eva's life…

"Does she tell you the lotto numbers?" He tried hard not to sound bad tempered and worry the poor woman further, but how could an intelligent woman such as Trish fall for Mystique's trickery?

"Yes." She laughed, and her eyes dipped only for a second as she tucked her short hair behind her ear.

"Why do you work here then?" He leaned into his seat. "You should have won that lottery by now."

"No, no." Trish moved to the front of the chair she'd held and perched on the cushion. "That's not how it works. I'll win some day, and when that day comes, she'll tell me. Till then I just have to go to her every month. The things she tells me, other than the lottery stuff, they are all…so…" She shook her head. "Like, you know how much I loved working for your father. When he retired, I couldn't bear to continue here. While I was going to leave anyway, I worked for your brother. And then you took over the company. Mystique advised me to work for you."

"Why?"

"I don't know. She said I'd love it here." She grinned her sweet grin, filled with admiration for him.

He hated himself some more for the many times he'd been rude to Trish.

"And what luck I listened, because look at me now." She swept her hands in the air. "I'm *so* happy here, Mr. Stanford. I'm happier than when I worked for your father." She chuckled.

"I'm glad you are." He had no heart to tell her what he thought about Mystique. "Thank you for sharing that with me."

She stood from the chair. "If you'd still like to meet her, I could bring her in now?"

He nodded. "And, could you announce in about…ten minutes, that my next appointment is here." He leaned farther into his chair and rocked back and forth.

Her eyes returned to shooting daggers.

He stilled. He cleared his throat. "Let's make that fifteen minutes." He grinned that grin again, because it had to work. And it did. She grinned back. "Yes, Mr. Stanford." She tugged at the door. "I'll be bringing her a coffee. Would you like one too?"

"Sure." He didn't need the caffeine, but the more he could shield himself from Mystique's emotional manipulation, the better.

***

How could anyone wear that much blue and of the same shade? Blue shirt, blue pants, layers and layers of strings with blue beads. If there were a name for that blue, Eva would know. *How is she so good with colors?*

Swimming pool blue? Yes, that's the blue.

The thought of his pool reminded him of Eva being terrified of even three feet of water.

As much as he would never force her to do anything she didn't set her mind to doing, let alone swim, her phobia niggled at him. What if whoever controlled the informant lurked around them all this time? What if this person waited for an opportune time to attack Eva? What if this person knew about her biggest fear? Did Eva have other fears? How had he never thought to ask?

He wanted to know everything about every one of her fears. *Now.*

He wanted to see her. *Now.*

That had become a self-defeating habit. At any time of any day he thought about Eva, he wished he could be with her right then. And he did make that happen any way possible. Heck, just the other day he'd walked out in the middle of a meeting, because he'd wanted to kiss her.

Maybe he should move his office to the thirty-eighth floor. They could add a stairway from his room into hers to cater to his sudden spurs of obsession. Or maybe he should convert the bedroom attached to his current office into an office for her? The bed would be gone, but they'd still have their desks, or the couch, or by that window. Eva's fingers splayed on the glass while he stood behind her, touching her, tasting her…

Those thoughts did him no good given that he'd somehow showed Mystique to the couch and sat in an armchair opposite hers.

By then, he no longer missed Eva; he craved her.

Though tempted to ask Mystique to meet him another day, he held back, remembering the tattoo Mystique had seen on the informant's arm that she had sketched for Trevor. They had compared that sketch with the one inked on the informant's hand when he'd met their undercover agent. The designs had matched.

"Water. That's why I'm here. I know that sounds strange." She laughed a light laugh, as though unsure of her words.

Of course, she answered before he asked, a way to lure him to believe she'd read his mind. But Mystique's perception had more to do with situational awareness than actual insight into his thoughts. Answering obvious questions before they were asked was one approach to confine and control a feeble mind.

"Water?" First it had been a boat, now water? Did she somehow know Eva's biggest fear?

But he wouldn't be asking her that. In fact, he wouldn't be asking or telling her anything she could use to move her story further.

"Yes, unhappy water," she went on.

"What about it?"

"Eva's in it."

He held back his chuckle. "Eva's in her office."

She narrowed her eyes. "You don't believe in what I do, do you, Mr. Stanford?"

"I do not. But please know I'm grateful you shared with us everything you could about that man who visited you in your parlor. Your description of his tattoo came in very handy. He won't be visiting you again." That last part he said anyway, though both he and Trevor suspected Mystique had been involved from the beginning. The informant may have been visiting her all this time, though they had yet to catch them together.

"Yes, I know."

Through tarot cards? Tempted to utter, but he held back.

"You've been watching him, haven't you?" Her gaze dipped to the coffee table between them and stayed set.

He didn't have to answer that. If anything, he wanted Mystique to tell him every detail about how she knew they'd found the guy. Either Mystique had insight about the informant's life that Clive did not, or she had once again tried to get him to lead her into his thoughts. He crossed his ankle over his knee and settled into his chair. He didn't want to reveal a thing to her. He could do this all day. "Why would you say that?"

A light knock on the door made them both turn their heads to look at Trish walking in with their coffees. She set the tray on the table between Mystique and him and left without a word.

"He didn't seem like he'd be able to get away with it for long. Not a smart guy," Mystique replied. "I mean, I know I met him only once. But, once is more than enough to gauge a person's traits, beliefs, lifestyle…*arrogance*." The way she'd stated that last character flaw, she disliked the informant more than she feared him. "You know what I mean?"

"Yes," he replied and dropped his gaze to the tray Trish had set between them. She'd added milk to both the coffees and hadn't brought in the sugar. He picked up a cup, set it on a saucer, and handed it to Mystique. "Please."

"Thank you." She watched as he reached for his coffee. She watched as he took the first sip. "There's something about you too, Mr. Stanford."

Something? A lot of things. The change his personality had taken after his experiences with Olivia, and then from his Special Forces and FBI days, would deter even a psychologist from any discussion about his traits. He could do without ever knowing Mystique's evaluation of him. Just as he should refrain from telling her what he thought about her preying on Trish. It bothered him that his nearly retirement-age secretary chose to spend her hard-earned money on Mystique. It also bothered him that he still didn't know the purpose of her visit today.

But before he could interject, and ask her to get to the point, she said, "You seem self-assured, confident, and…you are a genuinely kind man."

He didn't know how or why she'd made those conclusions about him, but he didn't care to ask, because, *get to the point.*

"It's going to be raining all this month. That's why I'm wearing blue. It signifies water."

"Really?" How is it that it didn't bother him that deep down he did want to know details about her choice of attire? He cleared his throat. "Why are you here?" *And what's in this coffee?*

"Happy month for most people, but not so much for others. You'll see the sun." She went on as though that made as much sense as anything else she'd told him so far.

For Eva's sake, for Trish's sake, oddly for Mystique's sake too, he tried hard to hold interest in anything she had to say. But his patience drained fast from her random chatter about water, about first impressions, about the weather. He cut a look to the dial on his watch and a surge of relief calmed his indifference. Trish should announce his fake next appointment any minute now.

Mystique continued, "But after that, there won't be any for a while. And it's all up to you to bring it back."

Of course, she'd added a riddle into this bizarre mix. Great. He directly asked the intent for her visit, and she threw him a riddle? Had he really held back from racing to meet Eva for this? "Listen. I respect that you're helping a lot of people with whatever it is you do. But—"

"Does this coffee taste okay to you?" She pulled her brows together and set her cup on the saucer.

No, it didn't. But he couldn't bear another diversion. "Coffee's fine."

"Your ex."

"I don't care about Silvia." The moment those words left his mouth, he regretted ever having spoken them. He had yet to meet a single person who didn't know his past with Silvia, or with all those other women the tabloids rumored him to have scorned. And Mystique wrote a monthly horoscope column for Izzy's magazine, which though not a tabloid, had covered a lot of useless details about him until Eva came to his life. Mystique, of all people, would have read every one of those details. But the fact that she led him into talking about his past, and that he somehow fell for that specific trick over all her other attempts, irked him the most.

He set the cup-heavy saucer on the table with an unrefined clank.

She flinched.

He didn't care. He never wanted to talk about Silvia.

Then why had he mentioned her? Maybe because she had yet to be erased from his thoughts? He had promised to find the sex tapes the informant had threatened Silvia with. One of those days when the informant had stepped out for his routine outing in the city, they'd searched the house. Other than unkempt furniture, clothing, bedding and few kitchen items, they found nothing they could connect the informant's activities to.

"Dark matter," she uttered.

He either laughed or choked, or a bit of both. "You're moving on to cosmology now?"

She gave him a blank stare. "Not *dark matter*. The matter, with your ex, the situation is blue. Dark blue."

Had there been any truth to tarot card reading, she should know colors weren't his thing.

Someone knocked on the door again.

She flinched again. Her coffee spilled into the saucer, but she held the cup steady, preventing it from splashing out into her lap. He picked up a cloth napkin from the tray and handed it to Mystique.

"Thank you." She dabbed the liquid that had spilled on her hand.

Trish peeked in. "Your next appointment is here, Mr. Stanford."

He hated to spend even a second more trying to connect, or at least somehow make the slightest sense of everything Mystique had said to him in the past fifteen minutes. But, come what may, he had to figure out how she fit into this story once and for all. "Please ask him to wait."

"Will do." Trish beamed a megawatt grin and clicked the door closed. She didn't know half of why Mystique had visited. But that she thought this meeting would benefit him somehow did make him want to soften his approach toward Mystique.

He cut to the chase. He went with his hunch. She didn't hint at his ex, Silvia. "How do you know about Olivia?" His stomach did a flip as that name left his lips. Olivia, his first girlfriend... Clive could never forgive himself for letting her go that night. Intoxicated, helpless, hopeless, she'd driven off the

154

cliff to her death.

"Was that her name?"

He wouldn't touch that.

"I feel it, Mr. Stanford. You don't have to believe in my work or my words, but I'm haunted by these thoughts, and I have to convey them to you. I like Eva, and I'd hate it if anything terrible happened to her. And same goes for you. I'm only trying to help, don't you see?"

His mood darkened. "No. I don't. And feel free to prove me wrong, because what I do see is that you're using your tarot card business as a decoy. You've already been informed that we're watching your every move."

"Yes. And believe it or not, I'm grateful for it."

Grateful? Did she mean bothered? Flustered? Missed her privacy?

"Had you met that guy, you would know. He is evil. And now, I don't know who is coming for us next. But, yes, thank you"—she half shrugged—"for the protection."

"Now why would you say that?" He couldn't deny his amusement at her slip of words.

She looked puzzled, so he explained.

"You just admitted to knowing I hadn't met the informant."

She blinked, continuing to look clueless.

"And why would you think there is someone else, other than this guy?"

She sat still. Whatever she hid from him, she

wouldn't for long. He'd make sure of that.

"Do you really not know how much trouble you've gotten yourself into by telling me that? Or is this, too, a part of your game? I'm going with the latter. Maybe you do know who that someone else is who's coming for us."

"I-I—" She licked her lips. A tight knot formed at her brow. "You know—" She set her saucer and cup on the table, her hands shaking as she did. "This was a bad idea. I'm sorry to have bothered you." She rose from her seat. "All I wanted was to convey to you that you'll be fine. Eva, too, will be fine. You will have this." She tugged at a few strands of her beaded strings and released them. They clapped as they fell back to her chest. "Happy blue. But you'll have a very unhappy one first. And I'm only trying to help."

***

Clive sat at his desk and compiled the video recording of his conversation with Mystique. Right before she'd walked into his office he'd leaned his cell phone against his laptop such that the camera faced them and documented while they talked.

Trish walked into his office yet again. He paused the video and set his phone on his desk, face down.

"So, how did it go?" She sounded cheery, exactly opposite of his present mood.

"What was in that coffee?" He snapped.

Her grin vanished. "Coffee." She blinked

clueless. "I-I mean, fresh ground coffee beans. I ground them myself right before I brewed them for you. Was it not good? I could brew you another cup if you'd like."

He was such a jerk sometimes.

"I'm—it was delicious, thank you."

She remained still and stared as though he hadn't finished his sentence.

"It went well." He forced a smile.

"Oh, that's wonderful." Concern in her expression from his earlier bad behavior lifted, and she, too, smiled. "And the coffee, Mystique brought those beans. It's called Twist."

She did? "Could you bring me the package?"

***

Clive tapped a message to Trevor: *Mystique.* He sent the video recording and minutes later, Trevor called.

"I don't know what to make of her visit," Trevor stated. "But I have many questions."

"Me too."

"You first."

"That thing about unhappy water. I told you what happened a few weeks back when Eva tried to swim."

"Right. Did you ever go back to your penthouse pool after that?"

Yes, after that family lunch in Eva's house. Clive's mood lightened, remembering their make out session. But they'd returned back to her home later that night. "With Eva, only once, but we didn't stay long. Anyway, either it's just a dumb coincidence that Mystique spoke about this today, or…" His gut wrenched, because everything about his conversation with Mystique seemed laced with ulterior motive, and he hated that he couldn't point to what that may be. There was much to decipher from that haphazard talk, and no guarantee any of their interpretations would be on the mark. He exhaled and leaned backward into his chair. "I don't know."

"Well, let's see, the only way she'd know about Eva swimming is by bugging your penthouse. Which is impossible, because you have cameras at all entry points. So how did she, or anyone else for that matter, get in without you knowing?"

"No one came in. I check the feeds daily."

"Okay. Then how about a drone?"

"A drone?" Clive chuckled.

"Why not? A recreational drone."

"Even if, they would have to hover it around at the exact time Eva was in the pool. Which again, I have cameras along the perimeter of the terrace."

"You have cameras along the perimeter of the terrace?" Trevor laughed. "The terrace that's on the fifty-sixth floor?" He went on, not bothering to hide his sarcasm. "Why? In case the informant drops from the sky?"

Any other time, he'd agree mounting cameras on top of one of tallest buildings in San Francisco came in handy in photographing outstanding views of the cityscape, and not much else. But he dreaded it would take only a second for someone to hurt the love of his life. "I'm not taking any risks where Eva's concerned."

"Okay. No drones. No bugs. How else then?"

"Either Mystique, or someone she knows, has known Eva's fear all along."

"I don't like the sound of that."

"Yeah? Imagine how that makes me feel?" Clive brought the ball of his thumb to his temple and massaged as though that should ease the throbbing tension that tugged him there. It didn't.

"You've got to force her to overcome her fear, man. Nina was a lifeguard for over ten years before she became a physiotherapist. Do you want me to ask her to talk to Eva?"

Worth a shot but knowing how Eva had already refused help from a psychologist, he doubted she would agree to disclose her anxiety to anyone, even if it were Trevor's girlfriend. "Let me ask her."

"Okay. Next. That part about you not meeting the informant. How did she know that? I mean, we've tapped her phone, we've followed her around. She has not contacted the informant, neither has she had a single conversation that we could flag as troubling. There is no connection to the life we think she leads, and what she said to you today."

That throbbing in his temple not only escalated

to an epic headache, it spread through his neck, his shoulder, down his entire body, and his muscles strained. Clive pushed back his chair and paced across the room.

"Right. And that thing about Olivia," Clive continued.

Olivia…Clive's stomach did that flip again.

Ryan, Eva's childhood friend, and Clive's once enemy, had called Clive this morning. They still had no clue who Ryan's secret client was, who had wanted Ryan to investigate why Clive's father had made sure none of the details about Olivia's death reached the media. They had suspected the client to either be the informant or his boss. While they had no evidence, they did get a good lead into investigating whether Olivia's death had been a suicide after all. All thanks to Lavato, the *Chronicle* reporter, who had left behind his press identification badge during one of his visits to Candy.

The informant had stolen the badge, and posed as Lavato that time he'd met Eva outside the coffee shop. He'd also posed as Lavato when he'd killed Candy, and later used the photographs to blackmail Lavato, threatening not only to tell his wife about his affair with Candy, but also blame him for Candy's murder.

Lavato had promised to hand over to Clive and Ryan an old news piece that a fellow reporter had written about rich kids who got away with murder in exchange for apprehending his blackmailer. The article was about Clive and Olivia but had never made it to print.

"I had a chat with Ryan this morning." Clive continued. "Lavato is ready to hand over the news article. Now, does Mystique know about what's in that article? And if she does, how?"

Trevor remained silent long enough for Clive to think their call had disconnected. Just as he was about to check, Trevor said, "I feel like we're so close to figuring this out."

"Yep."

"But I'm conflicted, you know what I mean?"

Not really. "Conflicted?"

"Have we fallen prey to a con, or is astrology real? She writes in *In Trend*, does TV shows and podcasts. She's famous, Clive. A lot of people cling to every word she says. Then why do I feel like we're the only ones trying to make her look fake?"

"We're not making her look fake. She *is* fake."

"Yeah, but what if. Right?"

"You're suggesting she is seeing the future in a crystal ball?"

"Not a ball."

What was inflicting this absurdity into his otherwise bright friend? "Don't tell me Nina's a believer."

"Dude, she's obsessed. Twist is literally the first thing she reads every morning after turning her alarm off. Really. Before she even gets out of bed."

"Twist?"

"Yeah, that's the name of Mystique's daily column."

"Like the coffee brand?" Clive picked up the coffee bag Trish had left on his desk and read the label more carefully this time.

"Yeah. It's one of many things she sells. I had never heard of it before I met Nina, and now, that's the only coffee allowed in our house. How do you know about it?"

He'd assumed Mystique had deliberately made Trish brew the coffee, as if she meant for him to relate to the name and add further mischief to their conversation.

But, on second thought, had she wanted him to taste the coffee because she knew Stanford Enterprise owned varied businesses and would perhaps be interested in buying hers? If she did have as much of a fan following as Trevor mentioned, it might be worth it to research the strength of her businesses after all. And if Mystique wasn't the culprit...

Wait. What? He returned his gaze to the muted gold label on the coffee bag. "I'm sending you a bag of Twist. Have it checked."

"What are we looking for?"

"Hallucinogens." Because how did he even once think Mystique wasn't somehow involved in this whole mess?

Chapter 15

Tonight would be the night he'd been waiting for. A lightless, lifeless, moonless night.

About a thousand times he'd paced around the house, until it grew dark outside. About a thousand times he'd peeked into the street, drawing a slight slit between the curtains to search for cops, Eva's bodyguard, or worse, her fiancé. That woman from the pier. That big man who'd ran to the light-rail. And somehow, worst of them all, that woman from the coffee shop who'd sat across from Eva. "Aunty Jamie," Eva had shouted. The way Aunty Jamie had stared at him, his blood grew cold, his breath halted, his confidence drained. He hadn't been able to force himself to approach Eva with that woman around. And then, he'd caught a glimpse of Clive, storming through the lobby toward the coffee shop. It had been best for him to flee before Clive took notice.

He'd had enough of this burden. He'd had

enough of this wait. He wanted nothing more than to return to his boat. His home. His money.

Thankfully, evening's darkness grew especially darker when two of the street lamps behind his house hadn't lit up. Had to be a sign. The time had come for him to sneak out. He dressed in black. He covered his face with a balaclava. He wore black gloves. He crawled out of the only window in the basement that faced the street at the back of the house. He didn't know whom to look for. Would they follow him in a car? On foot? He didn't know. But he'd bet his life, he would be followed. And for the moment, he didn't care, because he ran across the street, between the lifeless streetlights, across the neighbors' backyards, hid behind the bushes, and in the shadows. He ran and ducked. He ran away from his mother's house, once and for all. He'd never return. No matter what happened tonight, he would never, ever return there.

He ran up the ramp to his boat and over the deck, his every step resounding with the impact of his shoe against the wood. He reached the door to below deck, slid a key into the keyhole, unlocked, and swung it open. He stepped inside, yanked the door shut and latched all the latches as fast as he could. Spent from the frenzy that had started that evening he'd noticed the light in the navigation room, and continued until this night, he leaned his back against the door and remained there for a long time. He'd escaped from his mother's evil house, from the authorities that had followed him, and most of all, he'd escaped from his employer's never-ending threats. He closed his eyes. His chest heaved with every wheeze that brought him closer to catching his breath. *I'm home. I'm finally home.*

"Finally. Finally!" He laughed as he shouted and peeled off his balaclava.

He opened his eyes, but his heart nearly jumped out of his mouth when his gaze fell to the person sitting at the small dining nook.

"I was beginning to think you didn't want the money."

The snide voice gave away the person's identity: his employer, a woman, after all. How had it not occurred to him that she might be waiting for him, *on his boat*?

"How long have you been here?" He looked around the small space. His belongings were scattered about. He hated that she had rummaged through his things.

"Every evening since you saw my signal. But the way you ran back to your mother's, I knew it would take a while for you to return."

He gritted his teeth so hard his jaw hurt. "Where's my money?"

"In this bag."

His insides fluttered when his gaze fell to the zipped-up duffle bag. Its size just like from his imagination. He stepped toward it.

"Come have a drink with me. After all that you've been through, we should toast."

She brought out two glasses from a cabinet and filled them with a brown liquid.

He loathed her familiarity with his boat.

That changed his mind. He wouldn't spare her life. He plunged his hand into his coat pocket. He spun four fingers around the rope.

"Sit," she ordered.

He slid into the wooden seating attached to the table. Not because he feared her, but because he could pull the rope out of his pocket and ready it from under the table.

"To getting away."

He didn't completely understand her toast, but he clinked his glass and downed the bittersweet brown liquid. "Not bad."

"Yeah? One more then."

They downed the second shot too.

His heart cringed at her smug grin. *To getting away?*

Maybe because he could never understand what had possessed his mother to shoot and then stab her own husband to death. Maybe because he could never understand what had possessed him to strangle his own lover to death, his favorite girl—he had secretly loved Candy. If only he had told her.

If only he had told Eva. For all that he adored about Eva, for all that he'd wronged her, he stuffed the rope back into his coat pocket. Eva must know who had caused her grief all this time. Because given his employer's relationship with Eva… "Why would you do this to your…your own…"

Did I shake my head or did it shake on its own? Everything seemed to wobble.

"How could you do this to Eva?"

A cold chill ran through him. He shivered. Maybe the sweat from his frazzled escape from his mother's house had begun to cool. He tugged his coat closed.

166

The room swayed. The tide may be high.

The lamplight dimmed. The lamplight dimmed?

"Did you…" *drug me?* "But y-you…" *drank too.*

That grin, that smug grin. "Coated the inside of your glass, *you moron.*"

Those couldn't possibly be the last words he'd ever hear. The situation had turned out nothing like he'd planned. He was supposed to kill his employer. Better yet, he was to reveal to Eva who his employer was. But despite his best intentions, to come clean once and for all, to start afresh, to lead a decent life, he sat immobile, as though glued to the wooden bench, unable to stop the darkness descending on his vision, his body, his soul. "Eva…I'm sorry."

"Would you like to tell her that?" Her unsympathetic voice echoed from somewhere far.

"Yes…yes…"

"Sign here."

Chapter 16

Once again, Clive sat opposite Ryan, at the same table, at the same restaurant they'd met at a few weeks ago. They each wore the same white shirt and the same watch. Only difference, Clive's burger and fries remained untouched while he read every word of the four printed pages stapled together that Ryan had handed him.

Lavato wouldn't give up the news piece until they brought him concrete evidence about having apprehended the person who'd blackmailed him. But, Clive needed to get hold of the article before anyone else did. So, they'd changed their approach.

Ryan had kept watch on Lavato, snapping pictures of him to later use against him. Which, given Lavato's weakness for adulterous affairs, turned out to be an easy task, and he'd handed over the article to Ryan.

Though relieved that their plan to mine details

from Lavato worked, Clive's mood darkened at every accusation made within the document he read. "I can guarantee, Olivia *was not* murdered." His boiling angst may have been evident in his tone, because Ryan stopped eating at once and stared at him for a long second.

He set his food on the plate, brought a paper napkin to his mouth and wiped. "I believe you're innocent, if that's what you're getting at."

No. He had not been looking for an assurance from Ryan, or anyone else for that matter. He only cared for what Eva would make of the story. Especially those incriminating parts.

"I'm sure you can point out all the things that are true in here, and those that aren't. But, can you prove any of it?" Ryan had stated the exact dilemma that niggled at Clive.

No, he couldn't. And he hated that he couldn't.

Was Olivia murdered? No. At least that's what he believed given the state in which she'd left his driveway that night. A druggie. An alcoholic. A troubled child. Who drove off the cliff, either accidentally or to kill herself. Had that been the truth? Yes. Could he prove it? No.

Had Clive been her boyfriend? No. At least that's what he believed, given how she'd left him for Thomas, her photographer friend. She'd told Clive she didn't love him. She'd told Clive she wanted him out of her life. Yet he'd been the one she turned to each time she got herself into a mess. He was a friend. A close friend. A friend who cared. Had that been the truth? Yes. Could he prove it? No.

Had Clive killed Olivia? No. *No?* Hadn't he? He

should have asked her to stay. He had not. He should have stopped her from driving away that night. He had not. He'd let her go. Had that been the truth? Yes. Could he prove it? No.

"Are you telling Eva?" Ryan asked.

Had he meant to rub him the wrong way? "Why the hell would I not?"

As though to avoid the verbal punch, Ryan shot to the back of his chair. "Listen, man. All I'm saying is it's up to you to handle Eva. I'd like you to know that I'm not planning to tell her."

He understood Ryan was only trying to help, but Clive just wasn't in the mood for any of it.

When the restaurant door opened, a bell chimed, and Trevor hurried toward their table. He dragged the chair adjacent to Clive's and sat down.

He eyed Clive's food. "You planning to eat that?"

Clive pushed the plate and the cup of soda toward him.

"Sweet." Trevor cut his gaze between Ryan and him. Neither of them reacted and he said, "I know I'm acting like an inconsiderate jerk right now—"

"Acting?" Ryan teased.

"Yeah. Ha. Ha. Why's your plate all empty?" Trevor countered.

Ryan held Trevor's gaze. Keeping his face expressionless, he picked up his drink and sucked in through the straw.

"Nina's gotten into this let's-eat-healthy craze. I think she's making me eat bird food, man. Grains and shit." The depth of plight in Trevor's tone got Clive to laugh.

Ryan too, very nearly choked on his drink.

"So, yeah, I'm famished." Trevor took a large bite of the burger. "Mmm." He spoke with his mouth full. "This, this right here, mmm. Thinking that *this* is not healthy *is* not healthy. Right? Right?" He nodded, looking happy with his meal. "Anyway, what did I miss?"

They brought him up to speed. Though Trevor did have choice expletives for the news article's unfair offenses toward Clive, like Ryan, he, too, cleaned his plate. "Excuse me." He stifled a burp. "Nina's right. This can't be healthy." He sounded desolate as he stared at the empty plate. "I'm an inconsiderate jerk."

"Oh, don't spoil your post coital bliss with a sudden case of guilt." Ryan kept his tone theatrical.

Trevor shot him a look, and he grinned. He picked up the soda. "Do you always feel like that?"

"Like what?" Ryan asked.

"Like a giant asshole?" Trevor's drink gurgled, and he set the cup on the table.

Ryan laughed. "Good one."

"Right?" Trevor laughed too.

Any other day, Clive would have no qualms enduring Trevor and Ryan's banter. Today, he just couldn't get himself to shrug away from the fabrication he'd just read. "It's incomplete."

His friends sobered.

"You think there is a part two?" Ryan asked.

"Do you not? There should be a continuation leading to an ending. I mean, it tells you there's a victim and states all the possible suspects. Myself, Thomas her last boyfriend, other guys Olivia was seen with in school, her gymnastics instructor even, who was female, by the way. Can a media company print this without having proof of who did it, or, why they did it? They know I, of all the suspects, have the means to sue them to bankruptcy if their story is false. So, where's that proof?"

"You think Lavato has a second part?" Trevor questioned.

"No. He doesn't. He was quite shaken by our blackmail." Ryan added, "I'm positive. He doesn't."

"Okay, if not Lavato, then it's either the informant or whoever he reports to. This article does not end here."

Chapter 17

"They found him." Trevor bristled over the phone. "*In* the *damn* bay." He exhaled.

"Murder?" Clive asked.

"Suicide."

"That doesn't sound right."

"You don't have to convince me. They found a note in his jacket pocket. I have my suspicions as to how it got there." He huffed an unintelligible curse. "There was no way he would have spotted us by himself. This confirms the part about an accomplice." He paused for a moment. "We had him. We were so, so fucking close," he shouted.

Clive's blood boiled with the same frustration. He'd hated every second of what had appeared to be a never-ending month, as they waited for the informant to follow through on his threat and to make contact with Eva. Instead, he'd put them through yet another chase. Literally this time. The agents spying on him found him sneaking out of the only egress other than the main door of his home, his basement window. They followed. They ran when he ran. They ducked when he ducked. They followed him deep into the narrow, winding, cobblestone streets of China Town. But when the shadows lurking between the buildings grew longer and darker, they lost his trail. Their only hope, the tire screech that had echoed through the deserted late-night streets, must have been from the backup car that followed from intersecting roads and continued to chase the guy. But, yet again, luck favored the informant, at least during those final moments of their pursuit, because who would have thought the one street that set them close to chasing the guy, had to be the street blocked off for roadwork that night?

Clive let out a heavy exhale. "What does the note say?"

"Eva, I'm sorry."

"That's what it says?"

"That's all it says." Trevor grunted. "And hear this, it's sealed, as in one of those press-and-seal plastic food bags."

"And they didn't find such bags at his mother's?"

"Nope."

"Where did he live, Trevor? Obviously not at his mother's."

"We don't know. We asked around the neighborhood. Nobody knows. A good boy. That's what they call him. Can you believe that?" He snorted a light laugh.

"Why?"

"Because he took care of his grandpa. We visited the treatment home he lives in. Age related dementia is what the doctor said he has. We got nothing from the man. He owned a ranch and a farmhouse once, both of which he sold at some point. Half the money he deposited in the bank, which pays for his medical and stuff. Not sure what he did with the other half."

"Bought his grandson a place to stay?"

"Possibly."

"A boat?"

"Well, we didn't find any that matched our criteria. And we searched, not once, but three times." Trevor let out a sharp exhale. "So, yeah, that too, a dead end."

"Did you meet his mother?"

"Yeah. Got nothing from her either. Last she saw her son was the day she killed her husband. He never visited her in jail. Not once in all these years. But what I don't get is what did he do for a living? No bank account, no tax records, nothing. We found nothing. Did he use a different name? Was he just a petty thief who never got caught?"

"It makes no sense. Why Eva?"

"Yes. That's the strangest part. Why her? Why her father?"

"And who's his employer?"

They both fell silent for a long time.

"Anyway, you're telling Eva about the note, right?"

***

"Oh," was all she said when he told her about the informant's death.

Clive stood in Eva's living room, in front of Eva, watching her, waiting for her to elaborate. But she didn't. And he didn't like that she didn't, because, what might be racing through her mind? Yes, the informant's death in no way meant an end to her troubles. If anything, it only led to greater complications. And if it did make matters worse, did she know he'd protect her from whatever came their way? But what if she didn't believe that? What if she feared she would have to wade through the unknown by herself? "Talk to me, Eva."

She stared at him longer than normal.

She remained quiet longer than normal

"Please."

Still silent.

Maybe he should stop talking. Maybe that would bring her to speak her mind. They stood like that, facing each other, while neither of them said a word, except his mind willed and screamed, c'*mon, please, say something*.

She sighed.

Good…a sigh is something.

And silence.

"Well," they both spoke in unison.

"No, go ahead. Please," he offered, restless and desperate to hear her mind.

"Well—" Her gaze fell to the carpeted floor between them, as though she needed to contemplate what to say next. She sighed again and set her wineglass on the side table. "A man is dead, Clive." She shook her head at the floor. "A man is dead," she mumbled, and then paced from the family room toward the kitchen. When she returned to where she'd stood before, she stopped and faced him. "Even if he is the informant, he shouldn't have to die the way he did. Right? I mean—" She paced toward the patio door this time, stopped, and then turned around. "I mean, suicide? Over what, really?"

"He didn't die because of you." If that's what ate at her.

"It's not that."

"You don't believe he killed himself?"

"Of course, he didn't."

"What makes you so sure?"

"What was he apologizing about?"

What did that have to do with whether he'd committed suicide or not? "You lost me."

"Why was he sorry? For following me around? For pointing that fake gun at me? Would he really commit suicide over that?"

She sounded as though she didn't see in the informant the person who had distressed her all this time. "Those are serious crimes, Eva. He threatened your life."

"Yes, they are. But he didn't sound remorseful that last time I saw him, on the ski slope. If anything, he was enjoying that his plan to get me away from everyone else worked." Something shifted in her expression. Did she look worried? She played with the strings of her pajamas. *Nervous.* "All I'm saying is…"

The dip in her tone worried him. She thought hard about the situation. But he wished she wouldn't do that by herself without first letting him in on what bothered her. Because those were thoughts of worry, from realizing that though their ordeal with the informant had come to an end, his death led them back to not knowing who wanted Eva's company to fail, not knowing who killed her father, and the most troubling question of all, not knowing who would replace the informant and follow Eva next. Would that person play around like the informant had, or would he go straight for the kill?

"All I'm saying is his crimes don't justify committing suicide. He did say he didn't kill my father. And we've always thought there had to be someone else scheming here." She walked to him, plopped onto the couch, and picked up her wineglass. She brought it to her mouth but did not drink. "Maybe he came to the coffee shop that day because he wanted to take up my offer and reveal who his employer was. I'm not sure, and obviously, this is far-fetched, but what if that someone found out what he was up to and killed him?" She drew in a long sip and set the glass back on the table.

"Right?"

Clive sat down on the couch next to her. He tried hard to keep his tone calm. "Right."

"And we have absolutely no idea who it could be," she stated, not questioned.

He attempted to study her psyche through her expression. "We don't."

She didn't seem worried, which, though it did give him some relief, etched a renewed fear in his heart. He feared her boldness. He feared she'd come face to face with trouble, and instead of running as far as possible from it, she'd confront it. "We are continuing with the security I have set up for you."

"Of course." She leaned toward the coffee table and picked up the remote. "TV?"

He failed to muster a reply. Because, something didn't seem right. Did she really not want to talk about this anymore? Was she really not worried?

She met his gaze and held the remote in her hand, hovering her finger over the on button, as though waiting for his answer.

He half shrugged a *sure*, hiding away a *not really*.

She flipped through one channel after another. Typical Eva. A ritual she did each time she turned on the TV. She'd flip through the channels till she lost interest and then she'd hand over the control to him. He found comfort in knowing at least that much about her.

He circled his arm around her shoulders and pulled her to him.

She handed him the remote.

He searched and picked her favorite comedy movie for them to watch.

She rested against his chest and held on to his shirt in a tight fist.

The movie rolled through.

She should laugh. She didn't.

She should drink her wine. She didn't.

She should fall asleep in his arms. She didn't.

"Is it this weekend Carter and Izzy have planned the Santa Barbara visit?"

She exhaled. "Yep," she mumbled.

"And the weekend after is that repeat wedding-shopping day our mothers have planned for us."

"Yay." She sounded dull.

He smiled at her unenthused, dry tone. At least one thing he didn't have to pry out of her mind, their mutual boredom with anything related to the wedding planning. *Their wedding*, thanks to their crazy families, would be nothing like they wished for it to be.

Chapter 18

"Where the hell are you both?" Izzy and Allie shrilled through Eva's desk phone's speaker.

After their nightmare holiday in Tahoe, Eva had promised her friends a vacation-redo. They'd planned a weekend in Santa Barbara, visiting Stanford Spa and staying in Carter's vineyard home. She'd looked forward to her time away from her routine and wouldn't miss it for anything. "Waiting for Clive's meeting to end."

Allie groaned. For certain, Izzy had rolled her eyes.

"Why don't you go ahead, and we'll see you there?"

"But it won't be as much fun without you." Allie whined. "The plan was for us to drive together. Stop at scenic points. Take pictures. You know, vacation."

"And we have dinner reservations. If you don't leave with us, you won't make it in time." Izzy added.

Before Eva could answer, Izzy said, "Hold on."

Carter's voice filtered through the speaker, though she couldn't understand everything he said. Something about a helicopter?

And before Eva could probe, Izzy said, "Looks like Carter and Clive discussed an alternate plan. So, we're leaving now, without you, and will see you there. And please, please don't miss the dinner."

***

Eva stayed in her office and surfed the Internet for nothing in particular for an hour more till Clive messaged her that his meeting had ended. Relieved that they were finally on their way to catch up with their friends, she nearly ran to the elevator, rode up to his office, and ran to his office. She opened the door with a matched vigor and came to an abrupt halt when she bumped into this hard wall of muscle. Never had he waited this close to the door for her. She tried to tug away, half expecting the spot where her head met his chest to be hurting.

But he held her shoulders, not allowing her to move, and met her lips with a tight kiss. "Let's go?"

She nodded, taken aback at his desperate desire for her. But the grin plastered on his face made her suspect his forgoing driving with her friends might have been intentional. She narrowed her eyes.

"What?" He half shrugged as though he didn't have any such plans.

She held his gaze, because he knew *what*.

He brought her hand to his lips and kissed. "Too bad we couldn't leave sooner."

"Is it?"

He grinned some more.

She shook her head. "What are you up to?"

He didn't answer but continued to grin. He angled his arm. She looped her hand around his bicep and held there. They walked out of his office, through the long corridor that led to the terrace.

She could never forget that first time they walked this walk. That first meeting with Clive, that time when her company had nearly collapsed when Stanford had refused to renew their contract with S. F. Designs. She'd tried hard to stay focused in that meeting, but Clive had plans of his own for her then, as he did now.

Warmth rushed through her, remembering the first time she'd flown in a chopper with Clive. That first visit to the Stanford Spa, followed by dinner in Santa Barbara would forever remain one of the most memorable experiences she'd shared with Clive.

She continued to gaze at him. He continued to grin. They reached the end of the corridor. He set a flat palm against the door but did not push it open. He leaned in toward her and they kissed, a sweet, long kiss.

Just like that, whatever his plan, she didn't care to know. Because, all she wanted was right there with her.

He peered at her for a moment longer and then opened the door. Bright late-afternoon light momentarily blinded her while the strong wind that gushed to them caused her to sway toward him, just like she had that first time she'd stepped on this terrace.

Guess he'd planned to re-create that first time. She loved that he did.

He placed his palm on her lower back, steadying her. Though he'd touched her innumerable times, his gesture, still potent, rushed a longing for more of his touch. The same blue helicopter waited in front of them, blades already spinning.

"I need to fly to Santa Barbara. Join me." He asked with complete seriousness, just as he'd done that day.

"What? No!" She mimicked.

"We'll return in the evening. I mean, Sunday evening."

"No."

Clive softened his expression. An act, of course. "Eva, I'll be traveling for the next few weeks. We won't be able to discuss a probable extension of the contract until I return. Frankly, it might be too late by then anyway."

"I've never flown in a helicopter before." She kept her tone lifeless.

"I assure you, you're in *very* capable hands." He smirked.

"I'd vouch for that." She grinned.

As he did that day, the pilot handed each of them their headphones and gave Clive a thumbs up. This time however, her hands did not get clammy. Although her breath did catch in her throat from how much had changed between them since that first time. How many such sweet moments? How much togetherness? She was about to marry this man who'd swept her off her feet that day, as he did today.

"Oh wait. I forgot." She frowned. "There is *no way* I'm getting into this thing without the pilot. Are you even licensed?"

"I sure am." He went on effortlessly, as though he'd practiced these sentences over and over. "I could show you my papers if only you'd just *get in*." Their faces neared, and they kissed.

"I'm so happy for that day, Eva. I'm so happy for that elevator ride."

"Me too." They kissed some more.

He settled her into the seat but held her close for a moment longer and then he released her.

"Capable hands," she murmured.

He held her gaze as he buckled her seat belt. The look on his face, almost readable when he held her hand and touched the ring on her finger. Together…*forever*.

As it did that day, his touch left a fiercely tingling trail all over her. As she did that day, she wanted nothing more than to return to the moment in his arms.

***

She could lounge on this beach chair forever, in the shade of these rustling palm trees, while she stared at the glittering sea, drinking a cold, sparkly mixed drink crafted especially for them by the bartender at Stanford Spa.

"Where's Carter?" Izzy asked.

"Shouldn't you know?" Allie mocked.

Izzy rolled her eyes and plopped into the empty lounge chair next to Allie. "Well. As long as he's not here, I'm good." She picked up her drink and sipped through the straw. "I just wish I didn't come on this trip, with *my* boyfriend, to *his* vineyard." Izzy's pensive disclosure hit the emergency brake on Eva's reverie. She nearly heard her mind screech to a halt.

"Boyfriend?" Eva and Allie chimed.

Guessing by the stone cold look on her face, Izzy did not want to talk about how or why she'd used *that* word.

Her expression stopped Eva from prying. To Allie however, it was fodder to curiosity. "You wouldn't say things you don't want to say unless you want to say them, and you said it, so, *boyfriend*?"

Izzy sighed but otherwise remained silent, letting them wait for her to elaborate. She picked up her drink from the side table, sipped through the straw, and set it back down. "Carter wants to pick our relationship up a notch, and I'm blaming you for this." She pointed a finger at Eva.

"Me? Why?"

"All *your* wedding planning, that's why."

"First of all, I'm not planning my wedding, my mother is. And second of all…wait, he wants you to marry him?"

"Oh, dear God, no." Izzy scowled.

"What?" Now Allie scowled. "Why *no*?"

"I mean, not just yet. He wants me to move in with him."

"And what's wrong with that?"

"Okay, Eva. You're not allowed to comment on this anymore since you're about to get married, and I bet those rose-colored glasses aren't helping your thinking."

Eva pushed her sunglasses up to rest on the bridge of her nose. Yes, everything did take a happy rosy hue through them. "Do you like them?"

"I *so* do," Izzy replied.

"I do too. But, back to Carter and you. I agree with Eva on this. What's wrong with moving in with him? He's such a nice guy."

"I don't know." Izzy groaned and picked up her drink again. She pushed the straw aside, tilted the glass, and drew in a huge gulp. "Point is, I need him to keep with my twisted sense of relationship for a little longer."

Allie cut Eva a look. "Which is what, exactly?"

"No attachments."

"Ever?" Allie turned back to Izzy.

187

"For the time being."

"Did you tell him that?"

"Yes."

"And?"

"He promised our relationship would remain unchanged, even when we live together."

"See now...that's sweet." Allie nodded.

"No. That's impossible."

"Why?" Eva asked.

"Yeah, why Izzy?" That wasn't Allie. That was...

They stared in horror at the man who'd uttered those words. *Carter*.

"Why what?" Izzy asked as she settled into her chair.

He leaned in toward her and kissed her cheek. "Relax. Just messing with you, I don't know what you ladies were talking about."

If Eva didn't know to read the hidden meaning behind some of Clive's expressions, she wouldn't have been able to decipher his brother's look in that moment. Carter knew what they had been talking about. And Izzy's stubbornness unnerved him. But the gentleman that he was, he'd have the conversation later with Izzy, when they'd be alone.

And speaking of hidden emotions, Clive didn't look happy either. Had it been because Izzy sat to her right, Allie to her left, leaving no space for him to add a lounge chair adjacent to hers? He looked cute like that, as though deprived from holding her, touching her, kissing her…Eva scooted over to make space for him on her chair. In one second, he climbed over and slid next to her. And in the next, he moved her to sit between his legs, his back to the chair's, her back to his chest. He curled his arms around her, tugged her close, and rested his chin beside her neck on her shoulder.

"Happy?" she whispered.

His warm exhale confirmed his answer.

"Did you have fun golfing?"

"No."

"Why not?"

"I missed you."

His mumble sent a light tremor over her sun-warmed body. Clive must have noticed the raised bumps on her skin. He soothed with his hands, stroking the length of her arms, her upper thighs, over her bikini, to her bare stomach, trending upwards to her chest, but then he stilled. She didn't understand why.

Just as she'd been about to protest his cruel stoppage from pleasuring her, "Not here," he muttered by her ear.

Oh, of course. Yes. Not in front of their friends, and especially not all those things she wanted Clive to do to her.

"Let's get outta here?" he whispered.

Not wasting a second more, she swung her legs off the chair and stood.

"Where are you going?" Izzy probed.

Ahh…*where ever he takes me*, that's where. She mentally laughed at her innuendo. But seriously, what should she say? Clive? She cut him a look.

He held her gaze. "I'm famished."

Did no one notice the wickedness in his tone? She looked between her friends. Heat crept to her face. She didn't move an inch, hoping no one would notice her blushing either.

"Me too," Allie announced.

"But you just ate," Eva toned her words as calm as she could, but she also glared at her friend, so she could take a hint.

"A pineapple garnish from my drink is not lunch, Eva." Allie gave her a strange look. Did she guess what Clive and her were up to? Apparently not, because she went on, "I could eat a horse, the hooves and the tail."

"I'm not *that* hungry," Izzy added.

Oh, good. With Izzy out, Eva should be able to take Allie aside and convince her to change her plan. If only she could capture Allie's attention. She kept her gaze stuck to her friend.

"I'll skip the hooves and the tail," Izzy concluded.

Argh!

"We could eat right here." Before anyone else could object, Carter waved to a waiter. The poor guy didn't walk, obviously instructed by Clive to cater to their every need, he sprinted toward them. That would explain why her glass was refilled before she even noticed she had downed her drink.

The items on menu, their pictures and their descriptions, were so delectable, it would be hard not to pick something to eat.

And yet, Clive snapped the menu shut. "I don't feel like any of this. How about Vietnamese?" he asked Eva.

"Sure." She, too, snapped the menu shut.

"What? No," Allie whined.

"Yeah." Carter mimicked Allie's tone. But stated like the big brother that he was, "We'll have Vietnamese for dinner."

Eva darted a disheartened gaze at Clive. He stared right back, not looking happy, but not objecting to Carter's suggestion either.

Such went the remainder of their day. Almost as though neither Izzy nor Carter wanted to be left alone with each other.

After wine tasting at Carter's winery, followed by the planned Vietnamese dinner, Clive and Eva wished their party good night and hurried to their room. Just when they thought they were by themselves, Eva's phone beeped.

Izzy: *I had a nasty fight with Carter. All my mistake, of course. Cannot stay with him tonight. The resort is totally booked, so heading to a nearby hotel. Letting you know in case you look for me.*

Clive being Clive wouldn't let Izzy stay by herself. And there really weren't any spare rooms Clive could offer her friend. Which left them with only one option. Izzy spent the night with Eva, Clive with Carter.

Sunday, too, they were unable to snatch time away from the group. By evening, she couldn't tell if Clive was irritated by his brother or by the lack of a chance to be intimate with her. The latter, she suspected, from the way he laced his fingers with hers, and held her hand tight in his lap. They sat next to each other. Her thigh brushed against his. His elbow rested on the window frame. His face rested on his palm. Other than the occasional twitch in his jaw, he remained motionless, letting his gaze stay glued to the scenes passing outside of his window as Carter drove them to San Francisco.

It delighted her how much Clive had yearned for her. Their separation, though temporary, seemed cruel, but also quite sexy. And she craved him too. Her mind played a looping reel of how they'd ravage each other the second they got home. Her lips nibbling his. His meeting hers with matched precision. Her hands fisting his hair. His hands tugging and squeezing her in all the right places. Her insides leaped into a sensual dance of pleasure each time the visuals crossed her mind. Though she'd kept her emotions under control, the fact that Clive made no excuses for his intentions had her tickled. As a man not used to being deprived, he'd kept his conversations clipped since morning and had let a permanent scowl imprint his expression, deterring anyone from pressing him for more, all because last night had been the one and only night since they'd been engaged that they hadn't slept together.

She brought his hand up to her mouth. He shot her a wry glance. She kept her gaze connected with him, and instead of kissing, which he'd expect, she nicked his skin with a quick bite, to worsen his lust. The look he gave her, dangerous and gorgeous, a look he knew well would only increase her attraction to him. She liked that he looked at her that way.

In one quick motion, he tightened the grip on their laced fingers, and his other hand yanked, though gently, at her hair and tilted her head just in time to meet his needy kiss. Leaving her breathless, he pulled away only slightly, keeping her gaze captive with his.

"Want to fool around?" His gruff tone was wild enough for everyone else in the car to question if they'd heard him right but smooth enough to make her intensely desperate for him. Not like he'd care whether others heard him or not. But he did intend for her to sense his bolt of boldness. His mouth curved into a wicked smile proving her right.

"You're a savage."

"You love it."

Heat rushed to her face. She attempted to tug her hand away, but he pulled it deeper into his lap in that typical authoritative way of his, luring her to surrender. Unable to match his strength, she let him have his way. A light smile curved her mouth. She turned her head and looked away from him. He relaxed his hold on her hair and let his fingers twist and play with the length of her ponytail. She continued to look away.

He nuzzled his face into the side of her neck. His breath warmed her skin. "You smell divine." His voice, intimate and cajoling, as though an apology only for her to hear.

A surge of arousal roiled through her, and she couldn't help looking back at him.

How had they not figured out an excuse to separate from the rest, and taken the helicopter back?

He eased his grip on her, but he pulled her closer to him, placed a sweet kiss on her cheek, and returned to his scowl and staring outside his window. There was something sweet and precious about how much they needed each other. Nothing and no one could intrude when he held her like this. She tilted her head, resting it on his shoulder. The comfort in his warmth like a lullaby, she closed her eyes.

When she opened them, they'd reached her house. After waving good-bye to the rest of the gang as they drove away, she turned to face Clive. "Want to fool around?"

His soft laugh at his words she'd pitched back at him fluttered her heart. He slid his hand from her lower back around her waist and gripped her tight. No words were needed to describe their happiness from finally being left alone. No words were needed to describe their hunger that could no longer be contained.

***

They walked into her house.

He dropped their bags on the floor.

He took the keys from her hand and threw them to the floor.

He took her face in his hands and kissed her till they were breathless.

She breathed shallow and hard while she slid her fingers through his hair, over his shoulders, and down his muscled chest, to the hem of his shirt. She began to push the fabric up dying to touch his skin, touch him, everywhere.

Though they'd enacted nothing from her fantasy, their return home had every bit of the inseparableness she'd anticipated and so much more.

Not waiting a second longer, he picked her up like she weighed nothing and whisked her away to her bedroom.

The way he kicked opened the bedroom door, sexiest way anyone had ever opened any door...*ever*. From now on, she'd keep all doors near closed just to see him open them that way.

Her heart raced. Her body scorched. She gripped his shoulders tight, unable to hide her urge to surrender to her one and only, *Clive*.

Calm and collected, he set her down on the bed with purposeful leisure. The way his chiseled features remained unaffected and gorgeous and his muscles flexed with ease as though tensionless, it had to be the sexiest way anyone had ever gone to bed...*ever*. From now on, that was the only way she'd ever get into her bed.

She remained unable to tame her rising desperation, but then how did he look as graceful as he did even if his actions roared his precise intent? She studied his greenish-blues, and the depth of intensity in his lust filled gaze gave away his ache. He had become as deprived of her as she'd become of him. A thrill rolled through her insides and brought a light gasp to her lips.

Something about her gasp erased all trace of restraint in him. Before she knew it, his lips met hers, and devoured as though she'd become his only lifeline.

She moved her hands back to the bottom hem of his shirt and just as she was about to push it up, he caught her wrists and pulled back from their kiss. "Undress." The urgency in his tone betrayed what should have been a command.

Before she could muster a *say please*, she decided to teach him manners later. Because the erotic way in which with one swift move he tugged his shirt up his body, revealing his toned abs and broad chest, he'd just as quickly begun to peel off her clothes. His heated gaze traveled down every inch of her naked skin, lingering longer on her sensual curves. He unbuckled his belt but stopped zipping down his zipper mid-way when she unhooked her bra.

She loved how patiently, yet eagerly, he longed for her. She slowed her tempo. She slid one finger beneath a shoulder strap and let it fall off her arm. She repeated the same with the other, but then held on to the cups of her bra.

His gaze pierced hers.

She couldn't tell if she angered him or frustrated him, or maybe both. Lightning quick, he slipped off his pants, reached for her wrists again, and her bra fell to the floor. He pushed her hands behind her and locked them at her lower back. "You want to play?" he said tightly.

No. She didn't. Especially not now, because that would be self-torture when the heat in his eyes seared and raised her need to roll in bed with this gorgeous man. He pulled her to him. His strong body taut against hers, she longed for him to take her over the edge, and then some, in the exquisite way that he had her accustomed to. She licked her lips. Her need to give and receive pleasure heightened. Had she ever wanted him this bad?

A light smile curved his delicious mouth. He'd conjured at least one way to tease her, and she had to stop him from implementing his plan.

She tipped on her toes to rise as tall as she could and dragged her bare breasts against his chest in slow temptation.

His jaw twitched, and she smiled with perverse pleasure for having such an effect on him. But he straightened just enough to make his face unavailable for her to kiss. "You want slow?" he continued in that silky tone that conveyed he'd torture them both, but mostly her, because she deserved it. His fingers dug into her ass. He cupped and tugged her between his legs. Unabashed, he pressed his thick hot length against her, and she sucked in a clipped breath. Once again, her gasp defeated all trace of restraint in him.

"Fuck this," he muttered, and gripped and yanked the side of her lace thong. One moment it sank into her flesh, in the next it snapped apart.

Somewhere between their frenzy to strip off any leftover clothing, while also kissing and touching and gripping and tugging, they fell on the bed. He leaned on his elbows to keep his weight from crushing her, but the way he hovered on top of her, infiltrating her space, every inch of their skin in contact, made her body burn with wanting more. His hard muscle against her soft skin, his long strong legs holding her in place, her shallow breathing from his intense gaze, became the perfect amount of everything that pushed her blood to rush to her core. She became slick with want. She arched her back to press into his chest, but he bent his head and met her with the tip of his tongue. He licked her over and over, slow and unhurried…

"No!" Her moan conveyed her shameless plea, and he laughed a quietest laugh. "Really?" she fought, unrestrained, desperate.

He responded by drawing her in, hard and hurried. Relieved, she sighed, or moaned, or thanked; she couldn't tell, because she'd aroused a savage male. He had yet to touch her sex, and yet he'd revved her to such an extent, her muscles tensed in a way that meant one thing only, he had begun to push her to the edge. She closed her eyes. Her head fell back. "Don't stop."

He obliged her commanding whisper with deeper, rapid, ferocious pulls at her sensitive tips. His pleasure turned her on, to a point of no guilt, no restraint, no return. She arched her back not caring for the strain of her pose. His hands cupped and lifted her while his mouth feasted, not stopping even when she gave in, screaming his name in sheer bliss.

Panting, and all consumed, she opened her eyes to his stunning face.

The pain in his eyes, the tightness in his features, the hard sinew in his arms as he gripped her tight, conveyed how difficult it had been for him to detain himself all this while as she enjoyed herself in leisure. He needed her more than she could ever imagine. "Take me."

His heavy exhale conveyed how much relief her consent gave him. He spun her around and pulled her up. She rose on all fours.

"Tell me if I need to slow down." He wasn't teasing. As always, even at a time when she wanted him to take care of himself, her happiness remained his priority. She could never love this man enough.

With one hand he fisted her hair. The other he brought between her legs and pushed a finger inside her, then two, and started to plunge in and out, all the while circling her engorged nerves with his thumb, rubbing, pressing, pinching. She arched her back, letting him in deeper. Undone from what he'd begun to, once again, unleash in her, her limbs began to tremble. She started to lose all focus from being over consumed by what his skillful fingers did to her. As she welcomed the sexy haze that engulfed her, he grabbed her hips with both hands and shoved inside her. As always, he was too big for her in that first moment. She stretched for him, and a soft sound escaped her throat.

"Eva…" He sounded gruff. "Should I slow down?" He breathed hard and loud.

"No."

He paused as though unsure of her answer.

"Fuck me, damnit."

And he complied. His fingers dug into her hips while he stretched and claimed her. Deep. Intense. Raw. The need in his groan as he became desperate, breathless, pushed her into the oblivion again. He shuddered and folded over her. His chest along her spine, their bodies became one. Slick. Hot. Heaving. His grip on her hair tightened, yet he trailed the softest kisses over her shoulder, to the side of her neck, her earlobe.

Her wrung out body unable to hold up, her hands slipped on the silk sheet. Together, they collapsed.

Chapter 19

Clive sat at the edge of the bed, flexing his toes, as he oriented himself. He'd woken up several times through the night to make out with Eva, each time harder, rougher than the previous. What had gotten into them? Into her? She forced him to have his way with her. And he did. And she liked it. She wanted more of it. He was marrying a deviant fiend. And he loved her for it. He smiled.

Even after all that workout, he awoke energized enough to conquer anything, as though he'd had the best sleep he'd ever had. He glanced over his shoulder and found Eva, with the blanket covered to her ears, her expression calm and peaceful. All weekend he'd craved their togetherness, and despite his many tries, they'd stayed apart.

The reason for their separation, his brother's love life had taken a turn for the worse. Carter had always longed for commitment in relationships, but he never did meet *the one* to ask it of. He'd be what Clive imagined a perfect family man would be. A wife, a few children, a couple of dogs, a big house, would satisfy his brother to no end, but for whatever reason, Carter only met women who wanted the exact opposite. Clive wouldn't blame Izzy for not wanting what his brother offered, just like he wouldn't blame his brother for asking that much from Izzy. But it did hurt knowing his brother suffered in silence through the weekend. It seemed unnatural for Carter not to share his relationship troubles with Clive, and Clive couldn't understand why. The weekend being a replacement vacation for what they'd endured in Tahoe, maybe he didn't want to converse about his worries with Clive? They never did get alone time away from the others. Maybe he should ask Carter for lunch.

Clive picked up his phone from the bedside table to send his brother a text message. Instead, he peered at the screen. Eleven missed calls? Three from Ryan, four from Trevor, and four from his father. And several voice messages.

He tiptoed out of the room and quietly tugged the door closed to avoid waking Eva. He played the message from Trevor. "It's all over the news. Somebody leaked the story. They claim they know what really happened to Olivia. This is the missing part two Clive. You were right. There was more to the story."

He walked into Eva's study, opened the laptop, and turned it on. Seconds later, Clive was staring at an image of Olivia embedded in the news article.

"The American sweetheart who died before she ever lived," the caption read.

Her outfit in the photograph lured him to reconnect to the long-forgotten memory of the day she'd posed for that picture. That day when she'd tried on the pink glittery gymnastic dress.

"How do I look?" She twirled for him to gauge.

"Beautiful."

"Really?" Her face lit up with happiness, and she leaped into his arms.

She smelled of something sweet, mixed with the smell of chalk.

"Clive." Ryan's voice startled him to the present. The laptop, the news article, Eva's house, all returned to his focus. He turned his head toward the door, imagining Ryan had walked in. He hadn't. After Trevor's messages had ended, Ryan's started. Clive let out a heavy exhale and leaned back into the high-back leather chair. Had he ever been that relieved to hear Ryan's voice?

Each time Clive rehashed his memories of Olivia, his chest ached as though he'd been stabbed through his heart a million times. He'd hidden every detail about Olivia far and deep within the darkest recesses of his mind, terrified he couldn't live with himself if he ever resurrected them. And the news about Olivia, about him, had done just that. Remorse filled his heart. His guilt would never wane. If only he'd stopped her that night from driving drunk, if only he'd asked her to stay…

Ryan's voicemail played. "I confronted Lavato.

Took some hefty guys from my gym along. He didn't have the part two of the story we were looking for. He also didn't keep any copies of what he gave us. It isn't him. Positive."

***

The view from where he stood did nothing to improve his mood that had turned grim after reading the missing part two of Olivia's story. Bright blue bay, glass facade office buildings, and a miniaturized city buzzed unaware of his watchful gaze from the top floor of one of the tallest buildings in San Francisco. Any other day he'd take a moment and appreciate his sole reason for choosing this specific room to be his office. But today, today had been nothing like any day he'd ever spent in his office. He stared beyond the glass window, at nothing in particular. Burdened by his guilt-filled memories of Olivia's last days. Everything and everyone blurred from his life today.

A tender, familiar, hand on his shoulder made him spin around. *Eva.* Had she read the news? Had she read that part of the story he hadn't told her? Did she blame him for it? Regardless of what she thought of him, her merely being there alleviated his suffering somewhat. His gaze lingered on Eva's.

The worry in her eyes deepened, and the quietest gasp escaped her pretty pink lips.

When did she get here? He hadn't heard the door open. Had she already spoken to his father? He cut a quick look to the elderly man seated on the couch a few feet from him. His father looked years older today, as though defeated by the dilemma the morning had brought them.

Clive drew his attention to Eva.

"Are you okay?" she asked, his gloom mirrored in her expression and her tone. She placed her soft palm on his cheek, and he caught it.

His heart crumbled at her question. He turned his head and kissed her palm. He dragged her hand down to his heart and held it there.

He hated that he'd left home before she'd woken from sleep. After he'd read the horrid details into Olivia's death, he couldn't face Eva, or anyone else for that matter. He couldn't even leave her a note because what could he say? And what should he say to her now? Where should he begin?

"Olivia was pregnant." Each word that left his lips, made a deep cut in his heart, and he relived that moment when he let Olivia go.

"Thomas?" she asked.

He shook his head.

Color drained from her face.

He kicked himself for not being specific. "No one we know."

"Oh."

Olivia kept no secrets from Clive, even on her worst days, even after they'd broken up, even when she had started to live with Thomas. Each time she needed help, each time she needed someone to take care of her, Clive had been on her speed dial. Clive had been her go-to contact. Clive had been her pillar of strength at all times. Why then had she kept her pregnancy from him? He could have helped her. He could have done so much for her. If only she'd told him…if only he didn't let her leave that night…if only he'd asked her to stay.

Eva's eyes filled. Her face reddened. She seemed sad for him, maybe sad for Olivia too? She pulled him close and hugged him tight. He hugged back as tight as he could. He didn't know how or why, but somehow, only Eva could erase his pain.

I should have asked her to stay, Eva…

"Is it true?" Eva asked his father.

"Except that part about Clive being involved somehow, yes, the rest is true." Tension simmered under his father's tone. A vein twitched along the side of his jaw.

"S-so, did anyone tell the press what really happened?"

"Not yet."

"Why the fuc"—she cleared her throat—"*hell* not?"

A light smile formed in his father's features, deepening the laugh lines around his mouth.

Laughter. There had been plenty of that in his family, despite the many difficult bends in their lives.

"Olivia's family wanted details of her death kept secret," his father said.

"Why?"

"She was a star. They thought she could win gold at the Olympics. With all that fame and expectation surrounding them, they couldn't let her troubles go public. And after her death, well…they were the ones left behind, and they didn't want to be answerable to the world about how or why their daughter ended her life. And also because of what Clive had been to their daughter."

Though his father's expression went slack, his mouth curved downward, the gleam in his eyes reflected how proud he'd been of him. He'd told him that morning when the cops had visited their home to talk to Clive, and through the many years since, about how sorrowful he'd been of what had occurred to Clive at such a young age.

"Driving under the influence of alcohol was the part of the story they were willing to go with." He finished.

"You could have told me." Clive had clenched his jaw so tight, it hurt when he spoke.

"No. I couldn't have. She wrecked your emotions, Clive. Her cheating, her drug abuse, her alcoholism, were too much even for an adult to get a handle on, and you were so young. You'd taken too much blame on yourself already, any details about her death would have only made your recovery worse."

"I'll never recover from it."

"We all have our demons." The undercurrent of sadness in his tone made Clive worry. All these years his father had kept the news about Olivia's pregnancy to himself just to protect Clive from any further emotional damage, what else had he hidden from Clive?

"You were always there for her. She was a difficult child. She trusted you, and never once did you break her trust. You were there for her, Clive. Every single time she needed you, you were there."

"Except that one time when it would have really made a difference."

"You don't know that. Do you seriously believe if she had stayed that night, she would have told you any of this? She always came to you after the fact. She broke up with you, *after* she'd already cheated on you. She came to you for help, *after* she couldn't go home intoxicated. Even if you had stopped her that night, who's to say she wouldn't have driven off that cliff another day?"

They remained silent.

"We all have our demons." Clive mumbled his father's words. "What are yours?" He sounded caustic even to himself.

His father stilled, as though stunned by Clive's unexpected question. Then he sighed and leaned back. "All right." The confidence Clive was accustomed to seeing in his father returned as he turned to Eva. "I was supposed to meet your father the morning…" He paused for a second. He cleared his throat. "I was to meet your father the morning he was killed."

Eva's grip on their laced fingers tightened.

Clive's insides clenched. Taken aback by the unnatural calmness in his father's tone, given how he'd never spoken of the day his closest friend had died. How had his father kept that to himself all this while?

"I can tell you the exact three times in my entire life that I was late for a meeting. That morning was the third." His wince exposed how difficult it had been for him to come to terms with Eva's father's death. "Robin wanted to talk to me about the informant. He knew who it was and didn't want to speak over the phone. You never once think when you speak to someone it will be the last time you'll ever hear their voice."

He paused again.

"Before I could meet him at our usual go to coffee shop…" He closed his eyes for a brief moment, then shot them open and cut Clive a look. The strength in his gaze conveyed he was about to share *his* dreaded demon. "Not a day goes by when I don't reexamine the events of that morning. Not a day goes by without me imagining, and reimagining, over and over, how I could have saved his life. If only I had woken up earlier that morning. If only I hadn't taken the dogs for a walk. If only I hadn't spent that extra minute tying my shoelaces and had worn slip-ons instead. Because had I been on time that day, I could have saved his life. Maybe only for that one day. Because what about the next, or the one after? Though I know there is absolutely nothing I could have done to stop any of what had happened, I will still *never* forgive myself. I lost my only friend that day. And I'm at least partly to blame."

Clive's breath caught again. Not for his father this time, but for Eva. Her worry and insecurities about Clive's past had vanished, replaced by a tight jaw after what his father had disclosed. She didn't release her strong hold on his hand. She didn't move. She didn't blink. She stared at his father.

"Let's sit."

She remained still for a second, and then nodded. She almost stumbled as they walked toward the couch, but he held her up. They sat opposite his father.

Clive brought his free hand and cupped their already holding hands, hoping that might get her to break away from whatever uncertainties consumed her mind.

"He didn't give you the slightest hint who it may have been?" She said tightly. Her expression remained unreadable.

"No."

"You told me at the barbecue that day that you didn't suspect my uncle. Why?"

The barbecue? The day when she agreed to marry Clive? His father and her had spoken about her company that day? Why hadn't Eva told him that?

"Your father asked me not to tell Dave, not because he wanted to hide any of it from his brother, but because Dave meant everything to your father. And if anyone should reveal it to Dave, Robin thought it should be him."

"Why did he hide it from him at all?"

His father's gaze drifted to somewhere behind them. "Dave was traveling that week. Work related. And again, for whatever reason, Robin didn't want to speak about the situation over the phone."

"And why did he want to tell *you*?" she asked with a bite Clive didn't recognize. Did she blame his father for not being there for hers?

Eva's aggravation didn't affect his father one bit. He looked at her straight, and began to speak as though it had become unbearable for him to any longer keep secret the details leading to Eva's father's last days. "Because I know a few people in the FBI." He shot a quick glance at Clive. "Threatening letters are one thing, but when a company's stock is being tinkered with, it's no longer a local police matter, it's for the FBI to investigate. While your father had already reached out to them, he wanted to ask if any of my connections could somehow help."

"Why didn't he want to speak over the phone?"

It pierced Clive's heart how lost, clueless, and defeated she looked. He'd do anything, *anything*, to erase her agony.

"Your father became very paranoid near the end. He thought he was being followed. He didn't trust anyone, except me, Dave, and of course, Simon, his lawyer. And I can relate to how he felt. I was somewhat like that when the thing with Olivia happened. Before her father wanted to cover up the story, I was terrified for Clive. Then the press probed endlessly. For a long time they called Olivia's death a murder, and tried hard to link Clive as one of the suspects. I trusted only two people then, Clive, and my lawyer, John."

The depth of affection in his father's affirmation hit Clive hard. His own suffering was one thing, but for what his family had endured all this time for his sake, not once letting him take the blame, he'd forever remain indebted to them. He closed his eyes, tilted his head back till it rested on the edge of the couch, and exhaled slowly.

When he opened his eyes, for the first time since they'd sat on the couch, Eva looked at him. "The article still links you to her death." Just like that, her worry shifted toward him. And it only made him feel worse for her, because it had been bad enough for her to deal with the troubles she'd inherited, now she had his flailing reputation added to that list.

"It's time we reveal what really happened." His father said.

"Olivia's family is okay with that?" Eva asked, as though she'd read Clive's mind.

***

It had been a hellish few days. Reporters hounded Clive and Eva about everything Olivia. Had Clive gotten away with murder all these years? Would Eva still marry such a man?

From home to work and then back home, hiding from the world in tinted windowed cars, became their only outing for days.

Of course, it got worse when Olivia's family gave their account of the happenings, clearing Clive of any wrongdoing. The press continued to pester, questioning how and why Clive, his family, and Olivia's, lived with this tragedy at all. Though slow, the havoc eventually began to simmer.

One positive from all that, their mothers had stopped bugging them about planning their wedding.

Instead, their families and friends had secretly planned all the wedding necessities and hosted a surprise family luncheon for Eva and Clive's final approval.

Eva gawked at the dresses Claire had spread on her bed.

"I brought you my best three picks to choose from. So? Which one?" Claire's anticipation infected everyone in the room, including Eva.

Her friends wowed.

"They're...so..." Eva ran her fingers over the velvet dress in the same color the stone on her wedding ring had taken when sunlight fell through Clive's wineglass. How had they not noticed Claire listening in on their conversation that day? She'd picked the exact hue of pink Clive and Eva had mused for her wedding dress. "Stunning."

"It's called peony, and represents romance and grace."

Her friends *aahed*.

"Claire...I..." Eva's emotions welled. She cleared her throat. "I don't know how to thank you for..." Unable to finish her sentence, Eva did the next best thing she could. She leaned over to Claire and kissed her cheek.

Something shifted in Claire's otherwise jovial expression. "You know, given everything Clive has been through, we thought he'd never find that special someone." Color drained from her face. She looked pained. "I mean, everyone deserves to be loved, and Clive more than anyone I've ever known." Her gloom parted, and her signature happy smile returned. "And now, here we are, planning his wedding...*your* wedding." Claire brought a palm to her chest. Though she continued to smile, her eyes turned glossy. "It's you I have to thank for returning my brother, for bringing him back to life."

Her friends *aahed* again.

Eva hugged Claire tight. Because, really, how could she not love her soon-to-be sister-in-law?

After tears, and sniffles, and hugs, and laughter, they waited for Eva to take the lead. "Okay. Let's do it. I'll try the pink one first."

Chapter 20

Olivia's expression is exactly as he saw her that last time. Grim, bruised, brokenhearted. Wait. That's not Olivia. That's...Eva.

Eva. Who did this to you? Where was I? How did I let this happen to you?

Eva calls to him as she tilts to fall backward off a cliff. He let this happen to Olivia. He wouldn't let it happen to Eva. Her hand stretches toward him. Like with Olivia, no matter how hard he tries, he is unable to hold on. Eva begins falling into the cavern, screaming, "Clive...please...help me. Please. Please..."

Clive's eyes shot open. Winded and jolted from the worst nightmare he'd ever had, he blinked at a dull gray wall. *No, not a wall.* The otherwise white bedroom ceiling had turned gloomy from the predawn light that crept in from a slit between the curtains. Antique crown molding...they were in

Eva's house.

He stared at the ceiling as he caught his breath, while attempting to make sense of why he had conjured the nightmare at all. Eva's dreams were from a real fear, but his, especially the one he'd awoken from this morning, seemed baseless.

How convenient for his inner mind to have replaced Olivia with Eva? As if the haunting memory of Olivia's death hadn't been horrific enough. He fisted the edge of the sweat-soaked sheet that stuck to his chest and dragged it down to his thighs. A rush of coolness brought some relief to his heated skin.

How could he have let his thoughts morph to that convoluted state? Maybe it had to do with the recent findings about Olivia? The media had made hell over the news story. They'd followed him and Eva around for days. Though their frenzy had simmered after Olivia's family had made a public statement about their troubled daughter, the entire experience left a constant reminder for Clive to protect Eva not only from her worries, but from his past too.

To lose Olivia the way he had would forever remain an unforgivable turn of fate, but if anything were to happen to Eva...He tried to gulp, but his mouth had dried.

Like a movie, the scenes from his nightmare flashed in front of him. He closed his eyes shut tight. They stung from the unfamiliar emotions that had welled. He'd never cried before. Even Olivia's death hadn't rattled him as much as the thought of losing Eva had.

He turned to his side and pulled Eva close. She slept, calm, peaceful, and oblivious to the unrest in his heart that ached from how real the dream had seemed.

He pulled her closer yet and snuggled his face into the side of her neck. He breathed through ringlets of brunette hair...*her hair...her floral fragrance...*

He smoothed his hand down her arm...*her skin...soft and warm...*

He laced his fingers with her slender feminine fingers...*her ring...their engagement ring...*

Eva smiled in her sleep. Her smile made him smile. He had to kiss those full lips. So he did, and like in a fairy tale, her eyes fluttered open.

She crinkled her brows together. "W-what?" She sounded hoarse.

"You were smiling in your sleep."

"And why"—she covered her mouth with the back of her hand, stifling a yawn—"were you watching me?" She stretched her hands above her head, and the quilt slipped down, revealing her nipples taut under her silk nightdress. "Instead of you smiling in yours?"

"I'm smiling now. Does that count?" As his gaze ran over her body, a tight knot formed in his stomach. He couldn't bear to think about his dream, let alone speak it out loud, or worse yet, share it with the love of his life. He didn't know how, in that moment, he'd become the most superstitious person ever, and he shouldn't speak aloud what he didn't want to turn true. "What were you smiling about?" If he'd learned anything at the FBI, diversion would be it. Any other time, Eva would catch him with one look, but lucky for him, she'd just woken up and was a little slow in her reflexes.

"I dreamed of your pool again."

What? But she shouldn't have that nightmare here in her home. And...she smiled, as opposed to panted, or screamed, or awoke in a cold sweat, or a mix of any or all of those reactions? "And?"

"A hand plunged down to grab me...and...it was yours."

He peered into her hazel brown eyes. How much he loved this woman. How much he hurt by the mere thought of separation from her.

"Why weren't you smiling in your sleep, Clive?" she asked.

Between him and her, he'd always wish her to wake up that way, smiling. "Slept badly somehow."

"I can tell." She turned to face him. "Maybe I could help you relax?" She reached a soft warm hand toward the waist of his sweatpants.

Tempting...*very* tempting...but he had to talk to Trevor. He wanted every security detail to be extra vigilant around Eva today because...he couldn't stop himself from imagining that nightmare to be a premonition. He shut his eyes tight. *Don't even think it. Just don't.*

He grabbed her wrist and pushed her hand into the bed. He leaned over her and kissed her forehead. "I've got to finish something." Before she could say or do anything else, he jumped out of the bed and rushed to the bathroom.

***

By the time Eva dressed for work, Clive had alerted Trevor, Tom, Mike, and the Stanford Tower building security about kicking up their watchfulness a notch. But all that changed when Eva walked into the living room wearing a body hugging, baby blue lace sheath dress. She loved lace. He loved her in lace. Her lingerie always matched her clothing. And as he imagined her sexy curves draped in one of those sexy pieces—fuck the security details. Fuck work. Fuck everything else. "Let's not go to work today."

"What?" She looked at him like he was crazy. And she may have had a point, because he'd sure rush to insanity if he let her out of his sight and all because of that ridiculous—STOP THINKING ABOUT IT! He brought two fingers to the side of his head and massaged his temple.

"Are you feeling okay?"

No. I'm not. "Yes. Why?"

"You look like you're about to throw up."

That was it. Like a bulb lit up in his head. Maybe he should fake illness. That would make her not want to go to work. "Yeah. I think I have a fever." He tugged his tie loose.

"Really?" She slapped her palm flat on his forehead. "You liar." She laughed and turned toward the door. "I have that lunch meeting today, which you told me yourself that I absolutely cannot miss. Remember? We'll do whatever you want this evening. I promise. Now, c'mon, let's go already." She opened the door and walked out.

Without him.

She disappeared.

Without him.

"Wait." He ran to the door, swung it closed with a loud bang, and caught up with her as she walked toward his car parked in her driveway.

They drove in silence for the most part.

The closer he got to work, the closer he got to leaving her at her office, the more his insides knotted. Had she seen the future? Because he did want to throw up after all.

He held on to her hand as though it were the last time he'd hold her like this. "Let's elope."

"Let's."

"Really?" Because he would do anything, anything at all, to get her away from their familiar surroundings.

She shrunk farther into her seat. "Our families will never forgive us, though."

"I don't care. Let's elope today. In fact, let's go now."

"What?" She laughed her beautiful laugh. "No. I told you. The meeting. You should come along. We'll elope right after."

He ignored her suggestion. He didn't want to be

anywhere close to work today, or any place familiar to them, for that matter. He wanted to take her away from it all right now, and not after the meeting.

"There's that look again, like you want to throw up." She shook her head. Laughing some more she turned and looked out the passenger window.

When they reached the thirty-seventh floor, they kissed their usual *see you later* kiss, but he held on to her longer than he ever had before.

"Let me go."

"Don't leave me." He pulled her close. Every breath he breathed, he breathed her. Every degree his body warmed, warmed from her touch. Every beat his heart beat, beat because of her. He held her against his chest, tight.

"What's up with you today?"

That smile. His gaze lingered, as though it would be the last time he'd see that smile. Why couldn't he let go of that nightmare? He shook his head. "I miss you," he whispered.

She rose on her toes and placed a soft kiss to his lips.

Since their engagement, they'd spent every possible moment together. They went to bed together, they woke up together, they drove to work together, they texted each other through the day, yet, he craved more of her. Yet, he missed her, and today of all the days, he missed her more than ever. *Damn that nightmare.* He tightened their embrace some more.

Of course, she gave him another strange look.

Don't go, Eva. The elevator doors began to close. He didn't bother to hit the Open button, but she did.

And before he could say any more, she said, "The lunch meeting—"

"Skip it."

"It's that ten-year deal we're about to sign. These people flew in from Europe last evening just to complete this deal. Remember, you said this would be great for S. F. Designs and we must ensure this goes through? Also, this is the last deal I will have worked with my uncle. Remember? You know any other day I would totally play hooky from work." Her smile vanished for a moment but flashed right back at him.

His insides jumped, his heart raced, for *his Eva.* He'd love her forever, and forever thereafter.

"How about this, you come with me to the meeting, after which Aunty Jamie will be here. She's bringing us cake. Our wedding cake." Her face glowed with happiness. "We taste the cake, and elope right after?"

The elevator doors began to close again. Again, he didn't bother to hit the open button, but again, she did.

He cleared his throat. "Sure."

"To which, meeting, cake, elope…all three?"

Eva liked her independence. Her company was her show. And he would always respect that, no matter how badly he'd want to be with her. "Cake and elope right after."

She kissed him on his cheek. "Okay. Will text you when."

Don't go.

***

"She's not back yet." Tina's words amplified the unknown fear he'd carried all day. His insides twisted. He checked his phone to trace Eva's, but the GPS located her at her office. "She didn't take her phone?"

"No. She said she'd be gone for less than five minutes."

And she'd texted him, two in the afternoon, right before she left to meet her aunt. It had been over twenty minutes since.

"She should be back any minute now." Tina smiled. "While you wait, would you like something to drink? Tea, coffee…something else?"

"No, thanks."

"Izzy and Allie are also here, waiting in her office." She pushed the door open for him to walk in, but he remained still.

Eva's chair stood behind her desk, empty. Being in her office without her felt surreal. She should have been there already.

"Hey, Clive." Izzy and Allie waved.

He gave them a quick nod.

"What's wrong?" Allie asked, and she rose from her chair.

223

"Yeah, you look worried." Izzy walked toward him.

Not knowing what to answer, he shook his head and swiped his phone to call Tom. Maybe Tom had gone with Eva. But the elevator dinged, and Tom walked into the lobby.

Dark worry loomed in Tom's scowl.

Clive held his breath, clutching a desperate hope that Tom's gloom had nothing to do with Eva.

Izzy and Allie joined them in the lobby.

Tom looked at them all, and then back at Clive, and stood quiet as though uncertain whether he should speak his mind in public. His apprehension only worsened Clive's worry.

Clive rubbed sweat from his upper lip. "What's up?"

"Had I known Miss Avery had to step out, I would have escorted her to wherever she needed to go." Tom's brows came together. "She looked for me, and when she didn't find me, she went on her own. I'm terribly sorry, Mr. Stanford."

"Sorry for what?" Clive's insides dropped. He managed to force a smile. But Tom didn't ease one bit.

Tom cleared his throat. "I followed Miss Avery around the intersection, but then I—" he shifted his stance and cleared his throat again. "I lost her."

"That's not a problem." Clive patted his arm and forced another smile. "Eva's with her aunt." Though he'd assured Tom, his gut feeling pierced him that something had gone wrong. Eva should have returned already. She'd asked them to meet her at her office, which meant she had no other plans than to pick up the cake from her aunt.

"I see." Tom nodded. He tilted his head to the floor and continued in a cautious tone. "There were eight sedans. Three silver, four gray, one black, one red pickup, and one bus. One of the gray sedans was moving the slowest, so I concluded Miss Avery had gotten into that one. Although…" He paused, looking somewhat pale. His brows were still pulled together, and a nerve throbbed by his temple. "It didn't look like a car someone Miss Avery would know would drive. Tinted windows. No license plate. I'm—I have a bad feeling about this, and again, I'm terribly sorry." He shook his head. "Had I known Miss Avery would be stepping out, I would have waited for her in the lobby."

"Where was Mike?"

"He was on his break."

Tightness that had mulled in Clive's chest rolled up to his neck. His body heated to almost feverish. *Was it half an hour already?* Time ticked by at an uncontrollable pace. Had his premonition from this morning come true? He wouldn't let it.

He rang Eva's aunt and got her voice mail.

He rang Trevor and got his voice mail.

He rang the building security, asked them to keep the tapes from all the cameras they had in and around the building ready for him to inspect.

He strode toward the elevator to go look for Eva but halted when it dinged. Jamie walked in.

Finally. Clive exhaled his relief and waited for Eva to follow. But when she didn't, it was as though he'd been stabbed in his chest. "Where's Eva?"

"Huh?" Jamie winced. "I was about to ask you the same question." She extended her arm toward Clive. He didn't give a damn for social courtesies at a time like this, and yet he forced himself to bend down for a quick hug and a kiss.

"Looks like a party here." She grinned at them all. "How's everybody doing?"

No one answered.

"Take this, dear." She attempted to hand a round, white box to Tina. "This is Eva's favorite." She looked at Clive. "I can't wait for you to try it. Something tells me this will be your wedding cake."

"Eva went to meet you, like forty minutes ago," Tina blurted louder than he'd ever heard her speak.

Forty minutes.

"What? Where is she then?" Jamie looked around the room at each of them.

Again, no one answered.

"She didn't come see me. I waited—" She turned her wrist and gazed at her gold watch. "Yeah, for over forty minutes now. I couldn't find parking up front. Well, you know how busy that street is. So I waited for her around the corner. I did text her, so she knew where to find me."

"She didn't take her phone," Tina shouted.

"Oh, maybe she went looking for me? I didn't see her, though, when I walked in."

"What color is your car?" Tom asked.

"What?" She set the cake box on Tina's desk. "What has that got to do with—" She darted her gaze between Tom and Clive. She gasped and brought a hand to her mouth. "Oh, my God. Is Eva okay?"

"What color is your car?" Tom asked again. His dead serious tone could make a less prepared person tremble.

"W-white."

"There was no white car there."

"Where there?"

"On the street, where you said you waited for Eva."

"Are you calling me a liar, young man?" She took one step toward Tom and glared.

"No ma'am. Just trying to connect the dots here."

She furrowed her brows. "What dots? What's going on, Clive? Please tell me Eva's okay."

If only he could. "Tom saw Eva walk around the intersection. You didn't see her then?"

"Well, I waited by the hydrant. That was the only open spot. I had texted Eva to come pick up the cake in case I couldn't find parking. And the visitors' lot in this building is always full." She gave Clive a complaining look as though he should do something about it. "Anyway, so when the...the..." She snapped her finger. "What's he called? The ticket guy, well, you know whom I'm talking about. So, he came. Then I drove around the block and came back

227

to the street." She cut Tom a mean glare. "So yeah, I drive a white car. And I did wait for Eva on that *very* street," she continued with obvious irritation, but almost as though unaware of her own behavior. "In fact, my car is parked there now. Want to go check?"

Something crooked, almost evil in her expression, shot a nervous chill down from Clive's neck to his toes.

The way she uttered those last few words...*suspect*. But he had gotten a whiff of her alcohol-laden breath when she'd hugged him.

He shoved his hands into his pockets and tightened his fists, his only option to control the fury broiling in his mind. Why hadn't he forced Eva to stay home? Why hadn't he forced her to cancel that idiot afternoon meeting?

"That won't be necessary, ma'am." Tom smiled, looking genuine. "Thank you."

Ignoring Tom's attempt at a truce, she turned to face Tina. "Put that cake in the fridge," she ordered, but held her gaze at the cake box. Her expression changed again. She closed her eyes tight, and her skin crinkled. When she looked at Clive, her eyes had filled and reddened from emotion. "I'm sorry." Her lips trembled, and she brought a shaky, bony, hand to cover her mouth. She looked to Tom and then back to Tina. "I'm sorry." She shook her head. "I don't know what's gotten into me. Please, forgive my behavior. It's just that, I love Eva so much. And...I...I know how this looks, Clive." She splayed her hand on her chest. "But I could not

harm—" She shook her head. "How could I? I-I brought her cake…for her wedding…and I swear, I drive a white car." She pulled out a handkerchief from her purse and dabbed her tear-wetted cheeks.

Suspect or not, Clive would not rule anyone out before checking further. He couldn't shake his rage at anybody who'd taken Eva. He became a different man. One who trusted no one. Not Tina, not Tom, not even Izzy or Allie, and somehow, despite the cake, despite the tears, despite her affection for Eva, he just couldn't get himself to trust Jamie. Like Eva's father had asked of her in that last letter he'd left for her. *Trust no one.* Those words somehow became applicable to Clive. After all, Eva's father knew the ruse. That he might have been killed because of that knowledge alone made Clive more uneasy than ever before about where Eva may be at that very moment.

With hesitant steps, Jamie moved to the couch and sat at the edge of the cushion. "I can answer any questions you have, Clive. Whatever you need to know, however I can help to find Eva, I will."

But before he could ask anything further, she opened her purse and pulled out a steel, pocket-size flask. She took a long swig and tilted it at Clive, offering him a shot.

He shook his head, unable to grasp how she could take another swig of that drink when she already reeked the way she did. She continued to offer her drink to the rest of them.

"What is it?" Izzy asked.

"A secret."

"You might want to hold off on drinking." Clive ensured his tone warned more than suggested.

"It helps me behave, dear." She winked. Just like that, her unfriendly edge had vanished, she smiled her usual again. She brought her handkerchief to her eyes and dabbed the last of her tears. "But, you're right." She twisted the metal cap closed and dropped the flask into her bag.

***

Clive and Tom watched the security tapes the building guards were playing. Eva had walked out of the elevator into the lobby, waved at the security guards, and stepped out of the Stanford Tower. Moments later, she walked back in, spoke to one of the guards.

"Here's when she walks back in to tell me she left her cell phone in her office. She thought Tom or Mike would be right outside the door, but she didn't see either of them there. She asked me to text them both that she was going right around the corner to meet her aunt. And if any of them could, they should come join her. And now this is when I offered to go with her. But she refused saying she'll only be gone less than a couple of minutes."

Clive hated the timing of all the happenings. Eva forgetting her phone. Mike on a break. Tom had bent down by the car to check the tire pressure, an angle at which there would have been no way for Eva to spot him. And the worst of all, Eva refusing the security guard's offer to escort her.

They watched Eva turn left and walk toward the intersection. Tom followed. She turned left again and that was all that tape had captured of Eva.

"We don't have a camera on the side street?"

"No, Mr. Stanford," the guard answered. "There is no entrance on that street, so never saw the need for a camera there. But there's one on the traffic light."

"Yeah. Trevor is already looking into those tapes."

"I could ask around if anyone saw Miss Avery? Maybe one of the reporters followed her," Tom suggested.

"This can't go to the press."

"Absolutely not, sir. I'll keep my conversation casual."

Clive nodded.

His phone buzzed with an incoming call from Trevor.

"It's a one-way street," Trevor said. "And the only camera we have is facing the opposite direction of where Eva went. We cannot know which vehicle she got into, but we can run a trace on the cars that passed that street. Any specific vehicle we should be looking for?"

"Yes, gray sedan, tinted windows, no plates."

"Okay, hold on."

Clive's mind raced. He hoped Eva hadn't gotten into that car, or any other vehicle for that matter.

Maybe she'd walked into one of the stores and was on her way back. Or maybe she met someone she knew and went for a tea.

"Found the sedan but cannot see the driver's face."

Shit.

"Do you see a white Mercedes pass around the same time?"

"Oh yeah, a convertible. Drove past about five minutes before the gray sedan though. Sweet car. Eva's aunt's, right?"

Yes, Jamie drove a classy car, but the way she'd behaved today, Clive couldn't say she had much class. His conviction ingrained more than ever before, maybe because he was desperate to find Eva, or maybe because he'd never really liked her aunt, or maybe because of Jamie's crude reaction to Tom's questioning. "Do you see it again within the next forty minutes?"

"Hold on."

He almost wished Trevor would not see her car a second time. But something told him he wouldn't get that lucky.

"Yes, we see it again."

Shit. Her story fit. But Clive didn't want to rule her out just yet. It may be a stretch, but what if she had kidnapped Eva? What if she had an accomplice who had taken Eva while Jamie did the waiting by the hydrant and driving around the block as an alibi?

"Are there cameras on other traffic intersections around the neighborhood?"

"Unfortunately, not. They have it along the main street, but not the side streets. The gray car definitely took the side streets. We are now checking all the cars that drove past that intersection during those minutes."

"What about Jamie? Can you trace her way from the first time she passed the traffic light to the second?"

Trevor paused for a long second. "You think it's her?"

"I'm not ruling anyone out till I find Eva."

"Me neither. I'll call you back."

Clive ran out of the security room, through the turnstiles, and out of the building. Wind met him with a bitter bite of cold. He pulled up his collar and shoved his hands into the warmth of his pockets. He ran toward the street Eva had gone toward and met Tom and Mike heading back from questioning people at the neighboring stores.

"No one saw her," Tom updated.

"Do any of the shops have cameras?"

"Yes, the one right by the hydrant does. The camera faces the street, but it's only to scare off offenders, doesn't really record. The shopkeeper did see a white Mercedes wait there till a parking cop came over and talked to the old woman inside. She drove away after that."

Jamie's story fit again. He hated that it did. But his suspicion held. He wasn't ruling anyone out. He cut Mike a look.

"I'm terribly sorry, Mr. Stanford. I was gone

only for a couple of minutes, and I was in the building at that time."

"I know. I checked the tapes." Clive sounded harsh even to himself.

The fact that Mike went for his break at the exact time Eva had stepped out made him suspect Mike.

The fact that the camera at the Stanford lobby entrance captured Tom following Eva, but no other camera or person could account for what happened after they turned the street, made him suspect Tom.

He trusted only one person in the midst of this havoc. Just as he thought about Eva, his phone rang. He pulled it out of his pants pocket, wishing harder than he'd ever wished for anything in his whole life that it would be Eva.

"The white Mercedes turns off the main street." Trevor said. "Reappears at another main intersection. Disappears again after turning on one of the side streets. Eventually returns to the intersection by Stanford. All of that took about thirty-five minutes. The remainder of the time, about five minutes before Stanford cameras catch Jamie walking into the tower, she might have spent trying to find a parking spot."

"Can you see inside the car?"

"Not once. But I'm looking at these tapes in fast-forward, so we can close out some loose ends and think ahead. The guys here are analyzing further. Will take a couple of hours at least. What do you have?"

"Nothing. No witnesses. No cameras. It's a dead

end. It's a fucking dead end." The force with which Clive kicked the stone curb sent a piercing pain from his toe to his knee to his hip, making it difficult for him to set weight on his foot. But what hurt incomparably more was that no matter how much he'd tightened her security, no matter how hard he'd tried to keep her safe and hidden her from everything and everyone, his nightmare had still come true. He'd lost Eva. "Fuck. FUCK!" He punched the granite wall of the Stanford Tower. Blood trickled from his knuckles and dripped on the pavement. He'd lost Eva. How? How could he have lost her? Rain had started pouring with a vengeance, and never before had he hated winter so much. *Hope you're indoors. Hope you're warm.*

Chapter 21

Clive stared at his wristwatch. Nine-twenty in the night. Eight hours, twenty minutes, and twenty-two seconds since Eva went missing.

"I can have someone watch her," Trevor muttered to Clive and Ryan as the elevator doors closed, taking Jamie, Izzy, and Allie, down from Clive's apartment.

Clive let out a frustrated exhale and shook his head. "No."

They hadn't revealed to Jamie that until they confirmed the truth of every detail of her story, they considered her a key suspect in Eva's disappearance. Jamie had willingly participated in their questioning, though, as did Izzy, Allie, Tom, Mike, Tina, and Dave.

Trevor's team had checked the traffic tapes numerous times, measuring every second it should technically take for Jamie to circle the block and return to the street adjacent to Stanford Tower from where Eva went missing. With no visibility into the inside of the car, combined with the fact that several of the parallel streets were closed off due to road construction, and it would take her longer than usual to return to Stanford Tower, and the shopkeeper witnessing her being alone in the car when she drove away after being warned by the parking cop, they concluded Jamie hadn't lied.

They also traced the owners of the cars that had driven through that street around the time Eva had gone missing, but they'd found no suspects.

They questioned Mystique. Not a suspect.

They questioned everyone Eva had met that day. No suspects.

They questioned Trevor and Ryan too. No suspects.

They most definitely questioned Clive, longer than they had anyone else. A proven fact after all, the lover, the fiancé, the spouse, had almost always been the culprit. Every question they asked Clive, every answer he gave, brought flashbacks from when he'd been interrogated after Olivia's death. Fate had replayed its vicious joke, with amplified intensity this time.

Losing Olivia seemed like nothing in comparison to losing Eva. Harsher. Brutal. Inconsolable.

Izzy and Allie had agreed to leave only after Trevor promised to text an update every hour.

Dave and Julie, grief stricken and nervous wrecks, remained glued to Clive's living room couch.

Jamie didn't want to leave either, until Dave pushed her to rest, and promised that she, too, would get an update from them at the top of every hour. The woman did look shaken from the ordeal. She'd repeated the happenings to at least three officers and had offered to stay on in case they needed any further details. She glanced at her bag every now and then. Clive felt sorry for her alcohol addiction. He'd begun to believe her innocence, that she really did stop by Eva's office to hand deliver the cake, Eva's favorite cake. His gaze fell to the white cake box on the kitchen counter. *Wedding cake?* He almost heard Eva reply, "Wedding cake."

***

Trevor's phone vibrated on the desk, deepening Clive's already pounding heartbeat.

From years longing for Eva, his childhood crush, to his doomed-from-the-start, turbulent relationship with Olivia, his first girlfriend, and her suicide that haunted him to this day, to the gruesome experiences with Trevor during their time in Special Forces, to Eva's disappearance, he'd endured his share of the worst life had to offer.

Right?

Wrong.

Trevor brought his phone to his ear. "Officer Truman? Yeah, tell me." He shot Clive a quick look. "Uh-huh. Uh-huh. …Oh, you know what, hold on. Let me put you on speakerphone." Although he'd said that, he didn't set his phone on speaker for Clive to listen in to their conversation. Trevor's mouth fell open. He blinked. He paled. The dark alarm in his expression shattered every hope Clive had tried to cling to since afternoon…since the moment he'd lost Eva.

Trevor dropped his head, shoved his fingers into his hair and held them there. He remained silent for almost forever.

In less than a flash, every bit of happiness, every last hope, the slightest of desires, everything Clive had ever wanted from his life with Eva, shattered to innumerable minuscule pieces that could never be brought together again. Today would forever be the cruelest of days he'd ever lived. Because today would forever be the day Clive lost Eva.

Did they find Eva?

They did. *But? No. No. Please.* Clive shut his eyes tight, as though that would restrain his subconscious from suggesting the worst. He pulled in a deep breath, held it there, and chanted to himself…

Eva's fine.

Eva's okay.

She's okay.

Please, tell me you are, Eva. Tell me you're safe, you're alive. Tell me you'll come back to me.

Trevor cleared his throat and Clive shot his eyes open. When his gaze met with Trevor's, his dread was confirmed.

All those times Clive and Trevor had been on fierce missions, never once had he known his friend to look unnerved like he did now. Trevor slumped into a chair. His elbow angled on one knee, he leaned his head into the palm of his hand and glared at the floor.

Clive's insides did a sharp drop. Trevor's demeanor meant one thing only, they'd found Eva, but she was *not* okay.

This couldn't be happening. How did he let it come to this? From the time he'd met Eva in the elevator a few months ago, fifteen years after he'd last seen her, his darkest shadow remained the haunting possibility of losing her again, and this time forever. And he'd done everything he could for his brutal nightmare to never become real. So he thought.

"Y—yes, a blue dress."

Color had drained from Trevor's face. "Oh." His stare, cold, somber, exhausted every shred of hope, and conveyed the worst had happened.

"Y-yeah." Trevor cleared his throat again. "I-I'm here." A deep crease formed between his brows. "We're leaving now."

***

Minutes later, Clive and Trevor charged into the hospital lobby. The draft from the air conditioning felt warm on Clive's skin. Had his body become that cold?

"Officer Truman, this is Clive Stanford," Trevor introduced.

Truman may or may not have extended his hand to shake. Clive wouldn't know. Because he stood, in denial, unable to come to terms with the stark reality that they were to identify the body of a female who bore a close resemblance to Eva.

Despite Clive's relentless wishing and willing for this day to have a better end, his horrific nightmare had turned to reality. The punishing, vengeful fate had outdone them all. *But maybe it's not Eva*, his betraying heart teased with the dimmest ray of hope.

"Boyfriend?" Truman asked.

"Fiancé," Trevor answered for Clive.

Truman gave Clive a wary look. "It's not pretty."

Clive's teeth chattered. He clenched his jaw tight to get a grip on his anxiety, but nothing could reduce his pain. Though his mind, his body, his life had numbed, possibly forever, a sharp icy chill sprinted through him.

It's not Eva. He took a deep shaky breath. *It is not Eva.*

Truman stared at him for a long moment. "This way," he uttered in a low, grim, and sympathetic tone.

With heavy steps, Clive followed the officer toward the automatic doors that opened into a long, empty corridor. Sterile white walls and a matching tile floor reflected the impersonal, fluorescent overhead lights. And that smell, disinfectant mixed with whatever disease—*that hospital smell*—intensified his ghastly awareness of the only room at the end of the corridor, which they were headed toward.

Bile rushed to Clive's throat. He gripped the fabric insides of his jacket pockets tight. *It's not Eva. It's not Eva.* He chanted at every step.

They arrived at the dreaded room. Clive glared

at the floor. He couldn't peek through the viewing window. Because, what if…

It's not Eva. It's not Eva. He stiffened. His nails dug into his palms. His toes curled in his shoes.

Truman stepped inside the room, and Trevor followed, but at the sight of the outline of a body covered in a white sheet atop a metallic table, Clive remained paralyzed at the door.

Though he'd forced himself to remain in denial, reality hit him hard. He thought he'd crumbled to rock bottom when Trevor had updated him on the details of his conversation with Truman. But now, as he stood helpless, hopeless, and almost lifeless, the dark intensity of what he was about to witness stabbed through him. His heart sank farther, deeper, into an agonizing oblivion. Emotions welled, his throat closed, his eyes stung. *It's not Eva. It is NOT EVA!*

The coroner said, "I'm sorry you're…"

A sharp ringing ascended in Clive's ears, muffling everything and everyone.

There was a dull and distant, "Are you ready?"

"Clive?"

Trevor asked him something. Truman said something too.

Clive didn't want to hear.

He didn't want to think.

He didn't want to speak.

He didn't want to live.

Not without Eva. Never without Eva.

He wanted to race to wherever she was at this moment. He wanted nothing else but to be with Eva.

The coroner lifted the sheet, uncovering a young

woman's face. Clive's already shallow breathing came to a complete halt. He didn't know how or when, but he'd stepped in closer to the table.

Ringlets of brunette hair. *Eva's hair, her floral fragrance.*

The length of the body. *Eva's skin, soft, warm.*

Long feminine fingers. *Eva's ring, their engagement ring...*

He couldn't do it...he just couldn't look at her any further, and his gaze drifted to the blood stained blue clothing set in a rumpled pile atop a metal counter. The dress...blue...but...

His breath hitched. Because, that ring, *not* her grandma's ring. *Not* Eva's ring.

Clive's gaze darted to the woman's face. Heat rushed his body. His heartbeat picked up pace. His eyes filled. "It's not her." His breath wheezed. "It's not her." He took a few steps back. "It's not Eva!" he shouted.

Trevor groaned and threw up in a trash can. "Fuck," he yelled. "Fuck!" He kicked the metal container. When he turned back around to catch Clive's gaze, he was smiling, and also crying. "It's not her, man." He laughed. He wiped his eyes with both hands and brought them to rest on his hips. He exhaled and shook his head. "Thank fucking God, it's not her." He wiped his eyes again. He exhaled again. He laughed again. "She's alive. I know she is. She's waiting for us. I know she is."

Hopeful happiness had returned, but the abrupt release of pent-up tension drained all energy out of Clive. His knees wobbled, and he placed his palms flat on the wall to stabilize. For the first time since that afternoon, and the anxious evening that followed, Clive relaxed enough to hear again, to feel again, to sense again. While he absorbed the newfound reality that Eva was out there somewhere, alive and hopefully unhurt, his gaze returned to the woman lying in front of him.

Though an overwhelming relief that she was not Eva engulfed him, his heart still ached when he once again took in that face. Her skin, ashen, pale. Her bruised cheek. A lip, torn by a deep gash. Blood trickled out of the gunshot wound on her chest. Splotches of several dark bruises scattered about her body. Yes, she was definitely not Eva. And he was euphoric that she wasn't her. But his celebration was short lived, because she was somebody's daughter, somebody's lover, maybe a mother? How longingly he'd looked forward for Eva to return to him. Did someone yearn for this poor woman too?

Chapter 22

I'm swaying...I'm dancing.

But there's no music.

What's that? Leaves rustling. No, not leaves.

Lapping. A dog is lapping from a bowl of water. But, it's fast, too fast. It's not a dog...It's a dog. Clive's parents' retrievers? No. Not a dog.

Water. Hitting against something.

A boat? Yes. Water is lapping against the side of a boat.

I'm on a boat.

I'm on a boat?

My head hurts. My shoulders hurt. My entire body hurts. I'm going to throw up. I'm on a boat.

No...No. It's that nightmare again. It's all in my mind. I can stop my fear. I can control it.

I am swaying again. Violently this time.

The water is moving me.

This has to be a nightmare. I've got to wake up.

This is a nightmare, because, why would I ever be on a boat?

She tried to open her eyes, but they wouldn't budge, as though her lids were glued together. She tried harder. They remained shut. She tried again, and again, and a slight slit of an opening formed, followed by a sharp pain that scattered from her eyes to the back of her head. She cringed her eyes shut, avoiding the pierce from the brightest light she'd ever seen. But she opened her lids again, slowly this time, to a grayish-white fog. A blurry image formed ahead of her and sharpened with every passing second she squinted into focus. The image moved. What was it? Who was it? A woman…red lips.

"Aunty Jamie?" She winced from the pain that radiated from her throat. Had she swallowed a thorn? No, *tea*.

"Evie. I'm…I'm so sorry, dear."

"W-what?" Her voice cracked. As she cleared her throat, her gaze fell to her reddened wrists and the ropes fallen to the floor next to the wheels of a chair. Wheel chair? Had her aunt restrained her? Is that why she'd apologized?

Still numb from the effect of whatever may have been in that tea, thoughts rushed to her mind, but her body remained lethargic, unmovable, and dull. And then she began to recollect…

***

At two in the afternoon, right after Eva had finished her lunch meeting, her phone chimed from an incoming text from Aunty Jamie. *Can't find parking. Waiting by the hydrant. Come get the cake.*

Eva rushed out of her office, because one, she didn't want to keep Clive and her friends waiting, and two, she couldn't wait for Clive to try her favorite cake—their wedding cake, and three, did he really want to elope?

She'd hit the elevator button and pushed her hands into her dress pockets when it occurred to her she'd forgotten her phone. She'd turned over her shoulder, contemplating whether she should run and get it before the elevator got to her floor.

"Should I get it for you?" Tina offered.

The elevator dinged, and the doors opened. Eva waved to say both "nah" and "bye" in one gesture. She stepped into the elevator, turned around and faced Tina. "I'll be back in five minutes, maximum." The doors closed.

She stepped out of the elevator and walked through the lobby. Two security guards, who usually smiled and gave her a hello nod from behind their desk, obviously ordered to do so by Clive, came around their desk and approached her.

"Could we assist you with anything, Miss Avery?"

What had gotten into Clive today? She couldn't seem to take a breath without being asked by one person or another if she needed help. She didn't even want to know what he might have told them about her. For all she knew, they may already think of her as a pampered brat. Ah, well, whatever made Clive happy. "I'm fine, thank you." She grinned and waved as she walked past them, through the turnstiles, and out of the Stanford Tower.

It had become a habit now to look for Tom when she stepped out into the public. And he would always be right there, by Clive's car, parked by the entrance. Always. But not today. She found the car, but she couldn't find Tom. She should have brought her phone. She looked for Mike. He, too, should have been right there with Tom, but wasn't. Cold, harsh wind swept past her, and every hair on her body stood. She folded her arms across her chest, regretting not having worn her coat. She went with her third option and ran back into the Stanford lobby. A security guard approached her right away. She instructed him to let Tom and Mike know where to find her. The caring guard asked to accompany her. One moment she thought it would be a good idea, but she'd be gone for less than two minutes. And Tom would find her within that time anyway. No big deal. Besides, the more she hurried, the faster she could get back to the warmth of her office. She waved the guard good-bye, and rushed to her aunt, who should be waiting around the corner.

When she strode left into the intersection, she found a parking officer rolling his car parallel to the driver's side of her aunt's car. Eva did a quick scan of the road ahead of her, and dammit, no parking available, other than the space by the hydrant. Along several shop fronts, she wove her way around pedestrians surging over the cobblestone footpath. Wind blew at her with vengeance, just as Aunty Jamie pulled her car from the curb, and Eva sprinted. "Wait, wait."

Eva followed the car as it turned on a side street. She reached it just in time and swung her palm against the metal trunk, twice, and the car came to a halt. Eva ran to the passenger side door, pulled it open, slid into the seat, and closed the door right away, shivering as her cold body thawed in the warmth of the car. "Hey." She leaned over and hugged her aunt.

"Eva. Where's your coat? You must be freezing."

Her aunt hugged back. "Here." She hit a button on the dash that started the seat warmer under Eva. She hit a few more buttons, and hot air blasted Eva's hair away from her face.

"Ah, thank you." She sighed as she turned to sit facing her aunt.

A car honked behind them. "Oh, this city. Can't wait even a second," her aunt grumbled as she gave an angry look through her rearview mirror at the driver of the car behind hers. "The cake is in the back seat, dear, if you'd like to grab it. Let me know what Clive thinks about it."

"No, no, you should join us."

"I'd love to, but as you can see, parking is a nightmare."

"Want to circle around the block and see if we get lucky?"

"I doubt it, dear." The car behind them honked some more. Aunty Jamie gave the man a look angrier than before and added a slow shake of her head while at it.

"Now that I think about it, we should have left uncle's parking spot reserved for him for life, huh?" Though Eva had meant it in a lighthearted way, something shifted in her aunt's expression, and Eva couldn't gauge what had caused the change. "How's he doing?"

"Fine." She sounded angry somehow. "Golfing with his friends."

"What, today? It looks like it will start to rain any minute."

"Yeah. Going to be a brutal storm, they said." She shifted the gear to drive and moved forward. "I'll tell you what. The marina is only a minute away. Why don't we park the car there? You look like you could use a warm drink, and I have a flask of spiked tea in my bag." She shot Eva a quick glance and a grin and turned her attention back to the road. "We'll have some of that cake, and then I'll drive you back?"

"Sounds awesome. Let's do it." Eva rested her fingers against the vents on the dash, letting the hot air bring color back to her hands. "Oh, but I don't have my phone. And I asked Clive, Izzy and Allie to come to my office."

"Use my phone dear. It's in my bag." She pointed a thumb toward the back of the car. Eva turned and picked up a black leather bag from the back seat.

She dug through it. "It's not here."

"It's not? Did I drop it on the floor?" Her aunt shifted in her seat to check the floor beneath her seat, her control over the steering not steady. Eva clutched the wheel to straighten. "It's not here," Aunty Jamie announced as she checked the storage groove in her door.

"I'll look." Eva waited for her aunt to bring her attention back to the road and then bent sideways to inspect the back of the car.

"Hold on, let me park first."

Aunty Jamie halted the car in front of a white boat, from which a small ramp stretched to the walkway. She took her leather bag from Eva and pulled out a tall green flask and two porcelain cups.

A gust of wind shook the car, and Eva's attention narrowed on the boats lined up in the marina. They rocked from side to side in the turbulent water as though to herald the approach of that brutal storm. *Brutal.* Eva's insides did a drop. Memories of the lake by her grandpa's, memories of Clive's pool, memories of her many nightmares rushed into her thoughts.

"Eva."

Her aunt's concerned tone brought her back to the present.

"Are you okay? You look scared."

"Yes." She licked her lips. "I'm fine." She laughed, but in reality, she'd become uncomfortable in her own skin. Had the car begun to shrink inward, toward her? Or had it been her fear once again taking

251

over her mind? She inhaled a deep breath. She exhaled it. She inhaled again and a whiff of whatever her aunt had poured into the cups tickled her nostrils. "What's that?" She studied the dark liquid.

"Tea, dear," her aunt replied with an unnecessary rigidity. Something gripped Eva's chest. Maybe tea would bring her some calm.

With both hands, she took the cup. Warmth radiated through her cold fingertips, but she remained cold from the fear that had consumed her body. It niggled at her now that she should have waited for Tom or Mike to go with her. Or let the security guard come along. "Let's find your phone."

"Yes. But first, to being spontaneous." Aunty Jamie raised her cup and tapped Eva's.

Eva took a sip. And another right after. The spiked tea radiated through her, and she shivered.

"Now"—her aunt set her cup in the cup holder— "where is the phone?" She inspected the inside of her bag, the driver's side door once again, and just in case, the floor under her seat too. "Ah, there you are." She pulled her phone from a hidden groove under the armrest between the seats. "Here you go. Eva? Take the phone. Eva?"

Eva heard her aunt. She felt her touch. She saw the phone. But she couldn't move.

She heard her aunt again. She felt her touch again. But she couldn't see the phone. She couldn't see anything.

Her heart raced, or did it slow? Her breath, short, faint. She sank. Into the seat. Into darkness.

**

The tea…spiked…drugged? Drugged.

Her gaze fell to a round clock on the small wall in front of her. She squinted her eyes to read. Ten. Ten? She'd left her office at two. *Clive…*

Eva jolted awake to the smell of turpentine mixed with salty, fishy, cold humidity, and her surroundings came into focus. She was in a tiny room. Her aunt sat on a small bed a few feet ahead of her. Scattered about were several photographs, of her, of her with Clive, of her with her friends, of her when she ran in the park, of a man she didn't recognize, but she was in the background of those pictures too. The man…the informant?

They hadn't shown his photo in the news after they found his body in the bay. Is this you? She stared at a close-up picture of the man. His features resembled nothing she'd imagined him to be.

Wigs and facemasks hung on one wall. *He changed his look each time he met me.*

A wastebasket overflowed with crumpled paper. *Threat letters.*

Heat rushed to her face. She concentrated all her strength to wiggle her fingers, wiggle her toes, and though she moved only a little, a slight sensation from her extremities sprinted through her legs and her arms to her spine, her neck, her face. She shifted and straightened in her chair. All numbness began to recede from her body at once. Her eyesight returned to normal, and she glowered straight at her aunt. *You drugged me?*

As though having understood Eva's state of mind, Aunty Jamie's features contorted. Nervousness? Guilt?

"Tell them he killed me." She pointed a finger at the man in one of the photographs. "Will you do that for me, Evie? Please? I don't want Dave to know this. Please? It will break him." She licked her lips and her gaze dipped to the bed. "See, there's enough evidence here to prove he was the one threatening you all this time." She pulled out a few more photographs from a drawer that had already been set on the bed and scattered the prints on top of the rest. "Yes, these should prove it." She spoke to herself that time. "And see this?" She picked up a couple of photographs from the pile. "This girl. Candy. He killed her. See, these pictures of her. Naked. And this one. Dead. She looks dead, doesn't she? You'll tell them it wasn't me, right Evie?"

Her gaze met her aunt's, and Eva leaned fast and hard into the back of the chair. If she had to guess how a psychopath would look, it would be like her aunt looked in that moment.

"Where are we?" Just as Eva asked, her body swayed. The room swayed too, and nausea twisted her stomach. Her awareness returned to the fullest. Her mind cleared. "We're on a boat." She tried to gulp but her mouth had dried. "Are we on a boat?" Her heart pounded in her chest. She glared at her aunt for a response.

Aunty Jamie sprang to her feet and paced the

small space. She stopped abruptly and faced Eva. "Eva. Listen. I'm sorry, okay? I really am. It was a mistake. A *terrible, horrible* mistake. I'm so stupid." She slapped her forehead and left her hand there. "But…but we've got to protect each other. You'll help your aunt, won't you, Evie?"

Eva connected the events that had already occurred. Her aunt had directed the informant. She'd made him send her those threatening letters. She'd made him follow her. She'd drugged her and brought her there. She'd meant to harm her. But changed her mind. Why?

"Dave shouldn't know. Dave cannot know that I—I—" She shook her head. "I wanted him to own the company. He deserved to, don't you think? After all the years he worked with your father. But Dave never wanted it. Of course, I couldn't let go. You know?" She licked her lips. "It's not Dave's mistake. This is all my doing." She shook her head again. "Please, Eva. You'll help me get out of this mess, won't you?"

Had that been all she wanted, for her husband to take over after her father? And for that, she'd done all this?

"All you wanted was for Uncle Dave to take over the company?" she nearly screamed.

The look her aunt gave her, Eva stilled mid-breath. Realizing something had been horribly wrong with her aunt. Eva softened her tone. "You could have simply asked me."

"No. I couldn't," her aunt sneered. "You wouldn't have let go."

"For Uncle Dave? I absolutely would have."

"It's easy to say that now, Eva. And your uncle—" She huffed. "He would have never agreed to go against your father's will. It would have become a huge mess."

"And this is not a mess?"

"Actually no, it isn't. I'd have to kill you first. And get caught."

Psychopath. Eva gulped. "I don't understand."

"Your father didn't die by accident. I had him followed. I was trying to turn him paranoid, that's all. I assumed he'd think he was losing his mind, and hand over the business to your uncle. But then he found out it was me, and wrote the company to you, just to spite me." She grinned a devious grin. "Like I said, your father didn't die by accident. But they concluded he did, so I'm in the clear." She paused and her gaze drifted to the bed. "There's enough evidence here to blame *him* for all of this."

Him. The informant?

"I mean, look at these pictures. Proves that he followed you."

The informant.

"And here—" She pulled out a drawer from under the bed. "Tapes. Many, many tapes." They clapped against each other when she ran her finger over them. "Sex tapes, of all the women he's been with. And this one—" She pulled one out. "Candy," she read the title. "See?" The front cover had the same picture Eva had received from the informant, in which Candy lay dead on the bed. "This is his kill

256

tape, Eva."

"Whose?" She knew whose, but she wanted her aunt to reveal to her every minute detail of her wrongdoings.

"That idiot I hired to threaten you and follow you around." She covered her mouth with one hand as though only after the words had left her did she realize she'd confessed. Her face grew red. She winced, and tears trickled down her cheeks.

"Where is he now?"

She wiped her tears. "H-he's…" She licked her lips. "Listen, there's no time for this." She began pacing again.

"D-did you kill him too?"

She halted and faced Eva. "They'll come looking for you." She shouted.

"Mystique. Is she working for you?"

"Who?" Her aunt blinked. Something in her expression confirmed she had no clue who Mystique was.

"And Olivia. You have that missing news article Clive was looking for. It became useless to you once Olivia's family made the story public."

Her eyes widened. Of course, she had that missing news piece. "Eva! There's no time for all this. We've got to get our story right. We'll return to the dock. I can tell them someone drugged you and left you by my home. But you first have to promise to keep this all a secret. Dave *cannot* know this." She took a step toward Eva. "Dave can *never* know this." Her tone threatened.

Eva couldn't believe it had come to this. How could her aunt—*her* Aunty Jamie—who'd wanted to bake her a wedding cake—do this? And all these years Eva thought she knew her.

Eva trembled. She gripped the handles of her chair, anxious about what she was about to say to her aunt. "I can never forgive you for killing my father."

Color drained from her aunt's face. "You'll…" Her aunt took a quick step back. "You'll tell him the truth." She blinked. "You're going to tell, aren't you?"

Eva pushed up from her chair but almost sat back down when black spots rushed her vision. Her blackout lasted only for a second, but by the time she regained her strength, her aunt had turned around and run up the stairs.

How did her aunt bring her down there from the car? In a wheel chair, over that ramp from the boat to the walkway. Had she used the same ramp to bring her down there?

Again, Eva pushed up from the chair, but just as she reached the steps her strength drained. Again, her vision blurred with black spots. She held on to the railing for a long moment. The floor spun. She didn't feel well. Whatever drug her aunt had stirred into her tea had sucked out all her energy.

She climbed the stairs with caution. She stepped onto the deck. She stilled. Frightened by the sight ahead of her, all warmth escaped her. Not because of the fierce icy wind that blasted at her, causing her to wobble and grip the door, but from the rumbling storming sky, the grumpy evil sea, the merciless pounding rain—and her aunt, who sat precariously on the railing, her body facing outward, as though on the verge of jumping into the demonic sea.

The only light came from the navigation room and cast a dim glow on the deck. Even in the shadowy glimmer of the raindrops the light shone through, her aunt's intent remained unmistakable.

Her eyes wide, her face pale, Aunty Jamie looked hesitant whether to jump or not. She stared at the sea, and then at Eva. Back at the sea, and then back to Eva. Moments ago she'd acted as though she'd kill Eva, and now she wanted to kill herself? What had gotten into her aunt? She needed help.

"Please, don't do this. Get back in. Let's talk." Eva took a small step toward her aunt. "Whatever has happened, we can forget. We can move on."

"No, we can't. This has to end here."

"No. It doesn't."

The rising tide swelled toward the boat, making it leap with an unruly force, and crash right back to the water. Had Eva not held on to the door, she would have stumbled backward and fallen down the stairs. She swayed with the door, backward first, forward next, and by the time she'd regained her balance and cut her gaze to where her aunt has been seated, but she was gone.

"Aunty Jamie!" Eva screamed as she ran to the railing. "Aunty Jamie!"

In the water, her aunt moved her hands frantically, tying to stay afloat. "Eva," she yelled. "Please, help me. I don't want to die. Help me!"

Okay. But how? She'd do anything to avoid jumping into that water. And even if she did, how would they get back onto the boat? Her instincts kicked in. She found a ladder attached to the side of the boat and buttons adjacent to it with a down and an up arrow. She clicked the down arrow, and the ladder descended into the water.

"Swim to the ladder," Eva shouted.

"No. I can't."

"I've seen you swim many times. Now swim, dammit!"

"No! I can't. Please, Eva, help—" She disappeared under a rising wave.

"Fuck!" *Did she drown?* Eva's heart pounded in her ears. Her chest heaved. *Where is she?* "Fuck. Fuck!" She hit the railing with the palm of her hand. "C'mon. Come back up." She slammed the railing a few more times. "Please. PLEASE," she screamed. The water where her aunt had disappeared rippled and crashed with another wave, and then another followed.

One second, Eva was staring in horror at the rough, choppy, deep, dark liquid, and in the next, she dove into the mad sea. Icy water pierced at her like a million needles. Her temperature dropped. Chilled to her bones, she swam as fast as she could to where she'd spotted her aunt last. Right then, her aunt floated back up, coughing and splashing the water around her. Eva caught her arm and pulled her close. Her aunt clung to her.

"Eva…Eva…" She panted, she trembled, she

cried, all at the same time.

"You kn-know h-how to s-swim." Eva's teeth chattered.

"No."

"I've s-seen you s-swim."

"No."

"Yes." Every summer, in the lake by her grandpa's. Even that day when Eva had almost drowned. Is that why her aunt had brought her onto a boat? She knew her fear.

Her aunt stared somewhere behind Eva, as though she, too, was recollecting those summers they'd spent together. Picnics by the lake, those poker nights, the many times she'd taught Eva and her friends to bake, all those memories, all those moments when they'd laughed so hard that they cried. To Eva, her aunt had been a warm, loving, and caring woman, which made it that much more difficult to find that Aunty Jamie had a secret dreadful personality nobody knew of. Maybe not even her uncle.

"You know how to swim, now swim, dammit!"

"Y-yes." Aunty Jamie nodded.

"The water is too rough for me to tug you to the ladder. You're going to have to swim to it."

"No!" She tightened her hold almost choking Eva. "Don't leave me."

"I'm not leaving you. I'll swim with you. Let go of me." She tried to push her aunt away, but she clung to her tighter. "P-please, we've got to hurry."

Eva's body shivered, her teeth chattered, and the last of her strength drained. They had to hurry. "Go."

Her aunt nodded and slowly eased her hold.

They swam toward the ladder. Although they were close to the boat, each time they neared, angry waves pulled them back, forcing them to swim longer and harder.

Already weakened from being drugged, and the ordeal that had engulfed her since she'd awoken on the boat, Eva's fatigued muscles cramped each time her hands stroked the water. She strained the tips of her toes. She strained the tips of her fingers. She strained her neck, pulling breaths in as deep as she could. She'd nearly drowned once before, the horrific memory ingrained in her mind for life. She'd give her all to not sink below the water. *I can do it. I can do it.*

They reached the ladder. Her aunt climbed first. Eva followed after. She stumbled onto the deck. All her energy depleted, she sank to the floor and sat facing her aunt. Her chest ached each time she tried to catch her breath. For a long moment, neither of them spoke. The rain poured, the boat leaped, the waves crashed…

"Thank you," her aunt whispered. Her mouth quivered. She wiped her eyes with both her hands.

Eva stared at her, wordless, unable to come to terms with the extent of the evil her aunt was capable of.

Her aunt stared right back. As though she'd read Eva's thoughts, something shifted in her expression, and all signs of remorse vanished. The unfamiliar crookedness in her face shuddered Eva's nerves.

"Lock yourself in the navigation room. There's a phone in the drawer," she said. The disturbing grimness in her tone pierced at Eva.

"Why?"

Her aunt rose, but kept her cold, eerie gaze locked with Eva. "I'm afraid I'm going to hurt you."

What? Hurt her? But Eva had just saved her life. She almost wished she had her pepper spray with her. Regardless, she wouldn't let her aunt intimidate her. Besides, her best self-defense right now, was instigating regret. "Like you hurt my father?"

Eva held her breath as she waited for her aunt to become a nervous wreck like she'd become before. But her hope drained when her aunt smiled the coldest smile Eva had ever seen. "Lock that door." She turned on her heel and charged toward the stairway. Eva stared after her as she descended below the deck.

Reality hit her hard. Her aunt had meant every word. Eva pushed herself up from the wet deck, slipping as she did, but regained her stance and ran toward the navigation room. She swung the door open, and once inside, she pushed it closed behind her and latched the only lock above the knob. Her chest heaved as she tried to regain some normalcy in her breathing. She stared at the not-too-strong-looking plank of wood of a door, unsure if it would provide her any protection at all from her aunt, from the wind that howled from behind it, or from the rain that battered against the embedded glass window, because it rattled helplessly against the frame at each crack of booming thunder.

She couldn't fix the door. But she had to get out of the storm. She had to get off of the boat. She had to get on land. She had to get back home.

She spun around and glared at the navigation equipment. If she knew anything about boats, it would be from one of those shipwreck movies. *Titanic*. The thought sent a horrific visual of its sinking...this boat sinking. *Shit*.

Should there be a radio from which she could call for help? She looked around and found an old-style flip phone her aunt had talked about. She grabbed it quickly, with trembling hands, as though her life depended on it, because it kind of did. She flipped the cover open and checked the signal strength. Only one bar of the four had lit. Well. "One's better than none." Just as she'd been about to punch Clive's cell number into the cell, the boat leaped, and the last of the cellphone service vanished.

"No, no, no!" She gripped the phone tight with both her hands and stared at the barely lit screen. "C'mon! You're a phone. You call people. So, call people, dammit!"

Chapter 23

Clive's heart crumbled at the forlorn sight of Julie, Ryan, and Dave. He regretted not having given either Ryan or Carter a call on his way back from the hospital. Sure enough, they'd assumed the worst.

Julie sat on the carpet with her back against the couch. She'd pulled her legs to her chest, hid her face in her hands, and sobbed, inconsolable, for the return of her only daughter. She adored Eva. She loved Eva. Clive related to that.

Ryan stood facing the window. Water droplets trickled, sometimes slow, other times in a hurry, off the glass that had begun to fog on the inside. He didn't turn around, despite Clive and Trevor's return, as though he didn't want to know anything about the woman they went to identify. Because he didn't want to think it would be Eva, he didn't want to believe it would be Eva. Clive related to that.

Dave stopped pacing along the room, "Eva?" His eyes wide, his mouth agape, he stood still and desperate.

"No. Not Eva." Trevor answered.

"Oh, thank God," he moaned and slouched into the couch, looking years older than he had only minutes ago. "Oh God!" He placed his palm flat on his heaving chest. "Oh boy." He exhaled. Clive related to that.

Ryan still hadn't turned around, but his palm slid down the window and he crouched on the floor. He remained there, silent.

Julie sprang up from the carpet into Clive's arms. She hugged him tight and sobbed against his chest.

Trevor exchanged a quick glance with Clive. "Dave, I think you should go home and rest. These things usually take a while to get sorted. We'll keep you posted if we have any news. And Julie, maybe you too—"

"No." She pushed away from Clive. "I'm staying here till my daughter returns." She trembled as she spoke. "I'm not going anywhere till you find her, Clive." The hurt in her eyes, the anguish in her expression, the determination in her voice, Clive related to that.

"No." Dave shook his head. "If it's no trouble, I'd like to stay here, please. She's my only niece." He exhaled and leaned farther into the couch. "I've known Eva since the day she was born. I...I cannot...please, if it's no trouble, I'd like to stay."

Did he look worse than he did only minutes ago? The desperation in his voice, Clive related to that.

The door to his apartment opened. Carter walked in with their parents. His mother rushed to him and hugged him tight. His father followed.

"Sorry. I couldn't keep it from them any longer." Carter's usual carefreeness had vanished, his brows pulled together. He worried for Clive.

Clive gave him a nod, and just then, his phone buzzed in his pocket. He pulled it out. No phone number, and *unknown* flashed on his screen. A gleam of hope clutched his heart. *Eva.* But then a dark alarm wrenched him hollow. *Kidnapper.*

He shot everyone in the room a stay-here look, with the exception of Trevor and Ryan. They strode into Clive's study and closed the door behind them.

Clive gripped his phone tight and swiped to put the call on speaker. "Hello?"

"Cli…Cli…can…—ou…ear me?"

Though garbled, he'd recognize even the softest tone of that voice. No words could describe what that voice did to him in this moment especially. "Eva."

Trevor gave him a nod and got working with his team to trace the call.

"Ye… —s me."

Emotions blurred Clive's vision. He very nearly cried. "Where are you? How are you? Are you okay?"

"I…no."

"What?"

"I don…"

"I can barely hear you." He pushed the buttons on the side of his phone to increase the volume to the loudest.

"O…signa…po…"

"Where are you?"

She didn't respond.

"Eva?" He looked at his phone screen. The call had disconnected. "Did we get her?" he shouted to Trevor.

Trevor shook his head.

"Fuck!" He'd been desperate to hear from her, and when he did…the *damn signal*. Though his phone hadn't registered the number, he dialed back anyway. "The number you are calling is invalid, please check the—" He tightened his fists, ready to take a swing at something, *anything*. But when his phone crackled at how hard he squeezed it, Trevor attempted to take it from him. He stuck the phone to his chest. His irrational thoughts concluded letting go of his phone meant letting go of Eva.

"We need it to work," Trevor mumbled, low toned but an effective warning.

Yes, of course. Clive set the phone on the study table but continued to glower at it, willing hard for it to ring. And it did. He answered and set the phone on speaker mode.

"Cli…"

"Eva, tell me where you are. I'll come get you."

"On a bo…aun…Jam…"

On a what? And did she say Aunty Jamie? Clive, Trevor and Ryan turned to look at Dave. He couldn't be involved, could he?

"Are you safe?" Clive asked Eva.

"Yes."

Never before had he been so relieved to hear a simple *yes*. But as it had all day, luck tricked him yet again, and the call dropped. Once again, the connection had lasted too short a time for Trevor's team to trace Eva.

Clive shut his eyes tight and dropped his head. He couldn't let his frustration overrule his mind. He needed to channel his aggression into finding Eva. Into figuring out what she'd tried to say. He pulled in a deep breath and wiped sweat off his forehead.

He brought his gaze back to his phone and repeated aloud every sound, every syllable, every word he'd heard in that phone call.

"On a bo. Boat?"

"On a boat." Ryan repeated.

Trevor nodded. "Boat."

On water, without me. "Bad signal, so not the marina."

"Or the Bay."

"Signal the coast guard," Trevor yelled to his team.

Regardless of where the boat may be, it did little to alleviate Clive's dire thoughts after having witnessed the effects Eva's fear of water had on her. He had to find her. He had to find her fast.

His phone buzzed, but not from a call this time. The screen lit up from an incoming text from unknown number.

Unknown: *Signal's bad. Does this work?*

For the first time all day, his heart lightened. She always surprised him, his ingenious Eva. He read her text out aloud.

"Works!" he shouted and texted the same back.

Eva: *I'm on a boat.*

Clive: *Where?*

Eva: *In the sea, I think.*

"Shit!" he yelled.

Eva: *I see no lights, only a glow in the distance.*

Clive: *Sorry I'm not with you already.*

Ellipses flashed on his phone screen confirming that she was typing. He waited a long moment for her to reply, but she didn't.

He cringed, because only then did it hit him, what was he thinking reminding her that she was alone? She had to be terrified surrounded by all that water.

Clive: *Good that we're able to text. Means you are close to land.*

He hoped his last message could fix his previous gaffe, giving her some assurance, but she did not respond to that either.

Clive: *We'll find you in no time.*

He hated how unemotional text messaging could be. He hated even more that he couldn't be with her in that moment.

Clive: *Coast guard's on its way. I'll come get you very soon. I promise.*

Eva: *Thank you.*

Eva: *It was my aunt all this time. Can you believe that?*

His gut twisted. No matter how innocent and clueless Jamie had acted about Eva's whereabouts moments after kidnapping her, Clive had suspected her all along.

"Cold. Emotionless. Psychopath," Ryan blurted as he read over Clive's shoulder.

"We fell for her story, because it fit. Every detail checked out." Trevor sounded as exasperated as Ryan. "How could she have planned it so well?"

Clive shoved his hand through his hair and dropped his gaze to the floor. Eva had told him about Jamie's obsession with being perfect. How had he missed that one detail about her today? Her every action, every mannerism from this afternoon, made him only doubt her more. Especially after that drink she offered everyone. Sure, her speech had slurred a few times, and she'd asked for coffee. But had it been a ruse? A way to make everyone assume her to be a lightweight, but in reality, she'd been more aware than everyone else. He shook his head. "I should have gone with your suggestion to follow her." He hadn't, because he'd let logic overrule his gut feeling. "I fucked up. I fucking fucked up!" He punched his desk chair, and it swiveled on its wheels.

"We all did."

"Did he too?" Ryan turned to face the glass wall of Clive's study overlooking the living room. "Is Dave in on this?"

Dave sat on the edge of the cushion, as though he'd yet again been about to spring to his feet and pace across the room. He rubbed his hands back and forth over his knees. "Is she okay?" he mouthed to Clive.

No. But Clive nodded anyway.

"Is he playing us?" Ryan continued.

"Or did Jamie play him too?" Trevor added.

It had been about an hour and a half since Jamie left Clive's apartment. Did she go to the boat after?

Clive: *Is Jamie with you?*

Eva: *Below the deck. In shock, I think. She's afraid she cannot stop herself from hurting me.*

A cold chill sprinted all over his body. He had to find her fast.

"This means the boat was in the marina all this time. Till Jamie left. And then she took it out to sea. Eva was only five minutes away all this time, and—" Trevor shook.

Eva: *I've locked myself in the navigation room.*

Good.

Clive: *Look around for a weapon.*

Eva: *I already did. But no way I'm firing a gun at my aunt.*

Clive: *You have to if you need to.*

Eva: *No.*

Clive: *She is not your aunt anymore. She could come out of that daze you say she is in any moment now, and then what?*

She didn't reply.

Clive: *She's your kidnapper. You must protect yourself at all costs.*

Eva: *It won't come to that.*

Clive: *Please Eva*

Eva: *Fine.*

Clive: *Promise?*

Eva: *Promise.*

Eva: *Now, how do I drive this thing?*

Eva: *I mean, steer it.*

Eva: *Sail it?*

Eva: *Wait, no sails on this one. So, steer, right?*

She made him smile. He loved her so much. He missed her so much.

Clive: *You do neither. Find the radio. Should have a microphone attached to it.*

Eva: *Found it.*

Clive: *Look for a red flap with* Distress *written on it.*

Eva: *Found it.*

Clive: *Flip it open and press the button and hold it down till it beeps. This should send your location to the coast guard and any other boats around you.*

Ryan swung the door open and stormed toward

Dave. "Do you own a boat?"

"What?"

"A boat. Do you fucking own one?" Ryan shouted.

"No." He shook his head. "No, I do not. Why?"

"Does your wife own one?"

"N-No." The elderly man rose to his feet, shock written all over his face. "What's going on? Why are you asking me these questions?" He took a step toward the study. "What's going on, Clive?"

Whether Dave had been an accomplice or not, he left for Ryan and Trevor to figure out, because what concerned him the most in that moment was why Eva hadn't texted back? Had she pressed the distress button? Had it worked?

Clive: *Did it beep?*

No response.

Something had gone wrong, and the only possible explanation that rushed to his thoughts: Jamie had returned to the deck. He hated that thought. His muscles tightened.

Clive: *Eva?*

She didn't respond.

Signal or not, he hit dial, and she answered right away. But before he could say anything she yelled, "Aun...Jam...no. Ple...no... No!" The desperation in Eva's shrill tone corroded his insides. All those years of combat and hostage rescue experience, none of that mattered today. Never before had he felt this helpless and worthless. And he was to blame for this.

Letting Jamie leave his apartment unfollowed would forever be the biggest slipup of his life.

"Eva!" his voice trembled as he shouted into the phone.

She was right here, with him, on the phone, yet so far and unreachable. The nightmare he'd woken to that morning taunted at him. Once again, Eva had begun to slide away, and once again he could do absolutely nothing about it.

A harsh clank of metal bouncing off metal pierced his ear. She'd dropped her phone. Had Jamie hurt her? *Pick it up. Please pick it up.*

He turned cold, except for the side of his face, where his skin burned from how hard he pressed his phone against his ear. He couldn't let go. He wouldn't let go. "Eva!" His throat hurt, he shouted so loud. "Eva!"

Chapter 24

Eva dashed to the railing from where her aunt had once again dived.

"Aunty Jamie!" Panting, she shone the flashlight on the choppy water. Already soaked from her earlier swim, heavy droplets of rain drenched her more, while erratic wind froze her from her head, to her spine, down to the tips of her bare toes.

Her lace sheath dress clung to her as it held every bit of water that came in contact. Each raindrop burst on her bare skin, stinging needles as they dispersed. Her teeth chattered, every inch of her body hurt, and she could barely breathe. Yet, instead of running back into the navigation room to shield herself from the assault the storm had prepared for her, she gripped the railing as tightly as she could and scanned the savage water for her aunt. "Aunty

Jamie!"

Ferocious dark waves pounded the sides of the boat, one of which, higher and mightier than the rest, rushed over the railing onto the deck. Her tight hold on the barrier gave in to the brute force with which the boat leaped and swayed. She lost her balance and fell on her back. The flashlight slipped from her grip and rolled away. Icy water attacked and swept her across the floor, sliding her all the way to the other side of the deck. Her back hit hard against the railing, her only guard from being toppled off the boat into the ravaging sea. She ducked in agony, from the strong blow to her spine combined with the salty water that had filled her lungs. She groaned and wheezed, desperate to breathe. She coughed water over and over again. All energy spent, her body went limp. She coughed some more, until most of the water rushed out of her. Her chest ached, her air passages turned raw. Frantic to contain her choking heartbeat, she panted.

She had to get up. She had to find her aunt. Determined, she channeled all her strength to clutch the railing and pull herself up. But another unruly wave charged at her, knocking her back down.

"Aunty Jamie!" she cried, squeezing her eyes shut. Warm tears trickled down her near freezing cheeks. *Please, tell me you are* okay. *Please.* She wept. But the thundering sky, the cruel crashing waves, the ranting rain, remained her only response.

Reality set in. The moment she saw her aunt leap into the water, she knew it would be impossible to once again find her in this fierce storm. And even if she did, she didn't dare plunge back into that unkind sea only to once again rescue the one person she hated more than she'd ever hated anyone or anything before. Besides, her aunt wouldn't have jumped in to save her. Jamie stopped being her aunt the moment she'd filled her mind with evil against Eva's father. For a deceitful, cold hearted, murderer, drowning seemed an unearned escape. Jamie deserved much worse. That thought scared Eva but also liberated her from the guilt.

Frigid wind whooshed against her. Numbed from a potent mix of cold and fear, it seemed as though her body, her mind, had decided to acclimatize, to no longer feel. Instead, she awakened from her cycle of misery to what could be perceived as a compassionless and selfish conclusion, but much deserved at that. She should let go of her aunt and save herself.

The boat leaped again. Her back hit the railing again. The jolt, harder this time, sent a sharp pain down her spine to her toes. She curled them tight, a weak attempt to get a handle on the pain, but it made her that much more determined to somehow, someway, fight for survival.

She gripped the metal barrier with renewed strength, not allowing the storm to consume her. Somewhere between letting her body overrule her mind, and pulling herself up, she'd lost her fright. The gushing water, the treacherous rain, cautioned her toes to grip the deck at every step. And before another wave flooded the deck and propelled her off the boat, she ran toward the navigation room. She lost balance when the boat undulated another wild leap, but she grabbed the edge of the door to stabilize and swayed with it as it opened wide. She stepped into the room, pulled the door behind her, locked it, and ran to the loudly beeping radio.

She picked up the microphone and hit the talk button. She tried to speak, but her voice converted to one heavy exhale after another. She forced in a few deep rattling breaths, wincing each time as the pain in her back pierced with her every inhale. "He-hello," she shouted and released the control.

"Eva!"

"C-Clive!" Tears tumbled down her cheek and soaked her face.

"We lost you."

"Yes." She couldn't control her emotions. "Aunty Jamie…" she sobbed.

"Where is she?"

"Gone."

"As in?"

"She jumped."

"She's not on the boat?"

"No. But just in case, I've locked myself in the navigation room again."

"Excellent. Coast guard's on their way." Just as he'd said that, flashing lights appeared in the horizon. "And so are we. Switch to channel sixty-eight."

Sixty-eight, the same channel Joey, Ryan, and she used to set on their walkie-talkies while they played in her grandpa's backyard. Sixty-eight, her grandpa's house number.

Mayday. Mayday. Need medical assistance. Over.

In their childhood games, Joey had played a physician, code name Doctor Seuss, though not a real doctor, but at that time Joey thought he was, and Ryan's code name had been Sparrow, a detective.

She switched the channel on the radio.

"Is this Bunbuns?"

She laughed, she cried, she exhaled, all at the same time. How had Clive found out her code name? Her grandpa had called her Bunbuns. Cuddly, fluffy, those words well described her childhood body type.

"Bunbuns? Are you there?"

Her hand wobbled as she wiped the tears flooding out of her eyes. "Yes." She sniffed. "Who's this?"

"Eagle," Clive announced with a glint of smugness in his voice. *Before Eva could say anything,* "What the heck, Ryan." he yelled. "It's *never* okay to punch my arm. And especially when I'm flying."

"You picked Eagle just to top me," Ryan ranted.

"Why else?"

She wasn't out of trouble yet. They hadn't found her yet. She'd never been this stressed in her life. For certain they too concerned for her wellbeing just as much. But the fact that they chose to distract her out of all worry with trivial jest touched her deeply.

"Give me that." She didn't recognize the voice that accompanied the shuffle.

"And this is Cilantro."

What?

"It's me, Trevor."

"Cilantro?" Clive and Ryan spoke in unison and started to laugh.

"What *is* that? And *why* do you want to be it?" Ryan asked.

"Because then I top both you idiots, that's why. A wise woman once said 'Cilantro tops everything.'"

Her mind brightened at Trevor's reasoning. Memories of that wedding-planning lunch her mother and Diane had hosted in her home rushed to her mind. How simple the issues of that day seemed in comparison to what Eva had endured today. If impactful situations were to instigate a shift in the course of one's life, the extent of her ordeal today mingled with Trevor's choice of a code name would be the crystalizing reason for her life to change forever. She was a chef. She liked being a chef. She loved being a chef. She *would* be a chef.

The boat leaped, another hair-raising leap. But, it no longer mattered.

Lightning bolted close to her boat. But, it no longer mattered.

The rain poured heavier than before, erasing even the slightest glow from the city. But, it no longer mattered.

What did matter was how much she loved that moment, when her fiancé, her best friend, and her fiancé's best friend, now also her best friend, together, were on their way to rescue *her*.

"It totally does. Excellent choice, Trevor."

"Eva." Ryan sounded humorless. "Did you hit your head?"

"What? No. Why?"

"Because, Cilantro is the great choice? Wait, do you know what a sparrow is?"

"Or what an eagle is, because it's definitely superior to a sparrow."

Oh, their fragile egos. She rolled her eyes. "Cilantro smells nice."

For a long moment, the guys didn't respond.

"Hello?" She clicked and released the talk button a couple of times, to see if the microphone still worked.

They still didn't respond.

A renewed fear rolled through her. Did she lose them? Just as she'd been about to engage the talk button, Ryan came on. "Is it possible to speak the exact opposite of what you think if you've hit your head?"

"Why not?" Clive replied.

"She definitely hit her head."

"Definitely."

Of course, of all times, *now* would be when Clive agreed with Ryan. She shook her head. "I heard all of that."

"Excellent. Keep the updates coming. Concussions are no joke, Eva. Really want you to stay awake through this," Ryan added.

"What? I'm not concussed, you ass. Yes, Cilantro is an odd choice for a fierce FBI agent, but it's a really cute name. *Ass.*"

"You hear that, Clive?" Trevor chuckled. "I'm *fierce*. Rawr— Ouch. Eva, Ryan's hitting me. Ou-u-ch."

Guess they were back to punching each other or whatever. Were all men that silly when women weren't around? Or, especially, when a certain woman *was* around, because they'd do whatever they could to calm her mind?

She smiled. Her chest filled with air, her mind with hope, her body with a comforting composure, and for the first time since she'd awoken on the damn boat, she relaxed.

She needed this joyful banter with her family, her friends.

Family. Her smile widened. *Clive.*

Chapter 25

Eva set her phone on her patio table and her gaze cut to the date on the lit-up screen.

Today would be six months since her kidnapping.

Five months since Clive and she had married in a small ceremony at his parents' house in Sausalito. Claire and Mila, her makeup artist and hair stylist, had dressed her to perfection. Izzy and Allie wore whatever they'd each wanted, which in the end turned out to be the same style of dress. Her mother had cried, Diane had cried, both Joey and Trevor had cried—many happy tears. Ryan had brought a date, his ex-girlfriend.

Four months since their honeymoon at a secret locale, a private island only the two of them would ever know the whereabouts of.

Three months since Clive had moved into her house. Because, she'd said, "I'm *not* swimming,

Clive. *Never, ever* again."

And he'd said, "*Never, ever* again. I promise." Also, because Clive thought her house was cuter and cozier than his bachelor pad. But more so because many nights she woke up in a cold sweat, dreaming not of the lake, nor of Clive's swimming pool, but of being submerged in the ferocious seawater and unable to get back onto the boat. Regardless of where they slept, in her home or Clive's, she'd wake up in the middle of every night since they'd rescued her in the midst of the storm, staring at the ceiling. She worked on overcoming that fear, one night at a time.

That water, *that* boat. What a contrast to *this* water, and *these* boats she gazed at from her patio chair. The bay shimmered a peaceful, beautiful blue against the summery white sails. Birds twittered about the bountiful bougainvillea, and an occasional light breeze swept the steam off her jasmine tea.

How did she ever get so lucky? She smiled when a vision of her grandma flashed into her mind. She, too, had sat in this very chair every morning, and stared in the distance, smiling at nothing in particular.

And, like Clive, who read the words on his laptop screen with intense concentration, her grandpa, too, would be engrossed in the day's newspaper.

Clive stole his gaze away from the news for a quick second or two.

Stubbled jaw, disheveled hair, wrinkled jammies, and especially this morning, though he stared at his laptop more than he did at her, in this brief moment, his penetrating gaze captured her breath.

"The realtor found us some pretty good locations for our restaurant." He grinned persuasively. "Want to check them out today?"

She nodded.

She'd decided to continue to lead S. F. Designs, though only part-time. Her uncle returned to his old job and took over most of her work too.

Clive lifted her hand to his mouth, placed a light kiss, held it in his lap, and went back to reading.

How, again, did she get so lucky?

Before Clive returned to her life, if anyone had asked how she'd want to spend her mornings, she would have never been able to tell that this was how. And now, this was exactly how she'd want to spend every morning for the rest of her life.

She gazed at the sailboats and beyond. Her smile lingered.

Had that been why her grandma, too, smiled? For the everlasting happiness her lover had brought to her life. And the numerous possibilities of their future together.

Dear Readers,

THANK YOU for giving my debut series a chance. Hope you've loved reading Eva and Clive's story as much as I've loved writing it. It's been a long ride, and I've enjoyed every minute of it to such an extent I'm motivated to write many more stories. Wishing you'll want to read them all.

Please subscribe at

http://www.camelliahart.com/

to keep updated on newest book releases. I only reach out when a book is about to launch.

And if you are able to spare a few minutes to help me promote my work, greatly appreciate your writing reviews for my books, even a one liner helps, it's the stars that matter.

Thanks again!

Much Love,
Camellia

ACKNOWLEDGEMENTS

Nancy Cassidy, Penny Barber, Denise Pysarchuk - you are the best editors in the world! Thank you for your patience throughout this series, especially when we worked on this final book. Without you I wouldn't have even the slightest confidence to show my book to anyone, not even my pet cactus.

Pallavi, my adorable sister-in-law, and Maya, my dear friend – you are the best beta readers in the world! Can never thank you enough for helping with final touches to Killing Eva, which without your keen insight would forever remain an incomplete book.

My husband - you are the best husband ever! I love you more than words can say.

And the most selfless, dearest and sweetest people I will ever know - my readers, my bloggers, my social media sharers - you motivate and inspire me every day. Thank you!

ABOUT THE AUTHOR

Camellia Hart, a techie turned author of romance, lives in California with her husband, the love of her life. Other than writing her next romance novel, her hobbies include traveling, lazing on a beach with a good read, watching movies with happy endings while gorging on endless buckets of popcorn, red wine, and chocolate truffles.

Visit her website…

www.CamelliaHart.com

Follow her on…

Instagram: www.instagram.com/camellia_hart

Bookbub: https://www.bookbub.com/authors/camellia-hart

Goodreads: www.goodreads.com/CamelliaHartBooks

Facebook: www.facebook.com/CamelliaHartBooks

Twitter: www.twitter.com/HartCamellia